THE GUEST IS A GONER

A HUMOROUS, PARANORMAL COZY MYSTERY

CARLY WINTER

Edited by
DIVAS AT WORK EDITING
Cover by
COVEREDBYMELINDA.COM

WESTWARD PUBLISHING / CARLY FALL, LLC

THE GUEST IS A GONER

She's never believed in ghosts... until now.

As the owner of Sedona Bed and Breakfast, Bernadette Maxwell has always played up the rumors that her business was haunted. She's never believed it herself, even though she can't explain the odd odors that sometimes permeate the room or why a blast of cold air comes out of nowhere... until she has an accident and can suddenly see her resident ghost—her crazy, fun-loving, hippie grandmother, Ruby.

When a guest is found dead, the police rule it a homicide. It becomes apparent Bernadette is not only a suspect, but also in the crosshairs of the murderer. With no one to turn to for help, she relies on Ruby to assist her in a search for clues to bring the killer to justice.

Will Bernadette and Ruby find the murderer before Bernadette becomes the next victim?

CHAPTER 1

*H*ome Sweet Home.

After a long flight and drive, that's what I looked forward to, but that's not what I received. It felt good to exit the shuttle, stretch my legs and study my house, Bernadette's Bed and Breakfast, nestled in the beautiful Red Rock mountain town of Sedona, Arizona. The summer was almost upon us, and the sun shone brightly in the sky, warming my face. I sighed with contentment as I dragged my suitcase behind me up the walk. When I entered, I found my best friend, Darla Darling, who owned Darling's Diner here in town, waiting for me.

"Hey!" she called, standing from the sofa and setting down the magazine she'd been reading. "I'm so glad you're home!"

"Me, too," I said as she hugged me while I studied the living room.

Not a speck of dust on the fireplace mantle or side

tables, and not a cushion out of place on the two high-back flowered sofas facing each other, placed in front of the fireplace. She'd taken care of my house while I'd been out of town at my cousin's wedding in Louisiana.

"Everything has gone great," she said, tucking a lock of blonde hair behind her ear. She glanced over me as a mother would—head-to-toe. "You've got one guy up in room two, but other than that, it's been pretty quiet."

"Sounds good." I fell onto one of the sofas. "When did he check in?"

Darla took her spot on the other couch. "This morning. I haven't seen him at all. He's been very quiet. I think his name is Gonzalez."

I nodded, liking him without even meeting him. The last thing I wanted was a needy customer, and I actually appreciated the other two suites weren't taken. Yes, I needed the money, but right then, a bath and twelve hours in my own bed outweighed everything.

"Are you feeling okay, Bernie?"

I sat up and sighed. "I feel fine. It's like it never happened."

The 'it' I referred to was being struck by lightning. Honestly, I probably deserved it. While out of town for my cousin's wedding, they'd had a Voodoo priestess come out to release the soul of the caterer who had been killed right after the alligator ruined the ceremony. That's Louisiana for you. My daddy had told me not to attend the Voodoo ritual because horrible things could have happened, and he'd been right. A bolt of lightning came out of the sky and zapped me good.

Thankfully, I didn't suffer any injuries, but they insisted on keeping me in the hospital for two days for observation.

"I can't believe that happened to you," Darla said, shaking her head. "It's just so scary."

To put it mildly.

"It was, but I can put it behind me. I don't have anything wrong with me." I yawned loudly, hoping she'd take the hint. I loved my friend, but I wanted to be left alone. "Where's my cat?"

"She's pouting in your room."

The moody feline, Elvira, hated when I left her. The last time I'd been gone a few days, she'd torn one of my blouses—well, my only blouse—to shreds. Thankfully, we kept things pretty casual in Sedona and jeans and T-shirts were the norm, so I hadn't even been that upset. However, if she'd ruined one of my vintage eighties shirts, we would have had some issues. No one messed with my *Back to the Future* or *Breakfast Club* shirts.

"Elvira is weird, Bernie. This morning she sat on the couch and looked like she was tracking something. At first I thought it was a fly, but there wasn't anything there. It's like she was watching someone walk around. She gave me the creeps."

"I've seen her do the same thing," I replied. I found it unsettling as well, but most of the time it was easy to ignore her.

"You did have one problem while you were gone," Darla said. "I told one couple that the house was

3

haunted, as you told me to, and they didn't believe me. The next morning, during breakfast, they said they smelled marijuana, and they didn't appreciate me blowing smoke through the vents to try to get them high and hallucinate."

Despite my exhaustion, I burst out laughing. The thought of Darla smoking weed was almost as funny as me doing the same. We were both pretty straightlaced and the worst thing we did was have a glass of wine on Friday nights. Working out daily, practicing meditation and yoga, and eating well were our rules to live by. You wouldn't catch me dead polluting my body with marijuana, and certainly not Darla.

"Oh, for goodness' sake," I said, wiping my eyes. The strange odors that seemed to waft out of nowhere had never been explained, but being accused of something so ludicrous... well, that was a first.

"Yes. I couldn't roll my eyes hard enough," Darla said with a giggle.

"So what else has been going on?" I asked, standing and stretching my arms over my head. "Do you want some tea?"

Yes, I was tired, but Darla wouldn't leave until she spilled on everything I'd missed. Might as well enjoy some peppermint tea while we were at it.

"Sure. I'll come help you."

As I fired up the stove and put on the kettle, she told me about a desert Jeep tour that had gone particularly bad. "The whole family was in the Jeep while Jack was giving the tour."

"Where were they?" I asked. "Still on city streets or up in the mountains?"

"Completely off road. Anyway, Jack was giving his spiel and didn't hear the family ask him to stop. The kid, who was about six, threw up down the back of his shirt."

"Eww!"

"I know. It was awful. He ended the tour early and pulled into the parking area, ran to the back of the building, and began hosing himself down. To make matters worse, the family then decided to come into the diner and eat. That poor kid was green until he curled up in the booth and went to sleep."

With Sedona being a tourist town, the business owners kept in touch and also scrutinized the comings and goings of the visitors. Darla knew that since her diner sat next door to the parking lot of Jumping Jack Jeep Tours, chances were good they'd stop into her place if they finished their tour close to lunch or dinner. She and Jack often compared notes on his reservations so she knew how many people to staff in the coming days.

When I had customers interested in Jeep Tours, I always suggested they book through Jack, and he gave me a small percentage for the referral. I also highly recommended they eat at Darla's, especially if they raved over breakfast. The tourists didn't know it, but Darla provided my establishment with the morning meal every single day because I couldn't cook to save my life. If they liked her bacon, eggs, croissants and blueberry muffins, they'd certainly enjoy her tuna melt or roast beef sub. We were a close-knit community.

I grabbed some mugs from the cabinet and set them on the counter. The kettle whistled, and I poured the hot water over the peppermint tea bags. "Let's go back into the living room."

"Did your cousin ever end up getting married?" Darla asked, sipping her tea as we sat down.

"Yes. We talked on my way home from the airport, and they tied the knot last night."

"That's a crazy story, Bernie. I've never heard of an alligator ruining a wedding before."

"I know. The chaos was really something else."

We chatted a few more minutes, then my phone dinged, letting me know someone had made a reservation. I picked up the device and noted Mr. and Mrs. Thompson would be checking in later in the day.

"Are the other rooms ready?" I asked, hitting a button to confirm their booking.

Darla shook her head. "I didn't have time. I came here first thing in the morning for breakfast and checkouts, then ran over to the diner, and back here again. When you walked in, it was the first time I'd sat down in three days."

"Oh, jeez," I said, grimacing. "I can't tell you how much I appreciate you keeping me afloat here while I was gone."

"Of course. However, you do need to clean those rooms. The guy who checked in today took the last clean one."

"I better get up there and start scrubbing," I said, wishing I could simply crawl into bed.

"No rest for the weary."

"None. Do you think the new guy has any interest in sunset yoga?"

"I'm positive he doesn't," Darla said. "He's middle aged, a little on the heavy side, and came in with one of the smoothies from Sarah's topped with whipped cream."

A seriously broad generalization of who would like yoga and who wouldn't, but I was so tired, I was going to assume she was correct.

Sarah's Sensational Smoothies catered to every taste. I preferred the lemongrass and blueberry smoothies with extra probiotics, but she also offered the ones loaded with sugar, fat and flavoring, or as Jack called them, nectar of the gods. "Probably not a downward dog guy, then."

"I'm going to say no on that one.."

Sunset yoga was something I offered my guests during the spring and summer months if they requested it. Laying out yoga mats on the balcony facing east, I ran them through a forty-five-minute session. It wasn't something I advertised, but they were notified of the option upon check-in.

"I'll let you get to your rooms," Darla said. "I have to get back to the diner and make sure the dinner meal prep is going smoothly."

We stood and hugged once again, and I walked her to the front door. "Thanks again, Darla. Really."

"You owe me big time," she called as she waved over her shoulder.

And I did. It would be a tough repayment as well. She'd gone above and beyond what I could have hoped for.

After shutting the door, I listened to the silence of the house. I'd inherited the building when my grandmother died three years ago. It hadn't been a B&B then, but I quickly realized if I wanted to keep it and live in Sedona, I'd need to generate some income because I wasn't exactly bathing in cash being a yoga instructor. With three bedrooms upstairs, each with their own bathroom, and a master bedroom downstairs, I hung out my B&B shingle and began a little online advertising. To my utter surprise, I did quite well.

A small part of me wanted to sell the house, but I couldn't bring myself to do it. My grandmother had been beautifully crazy and I had many fond memories of her that made me smile. I wasn't quite ready to say goodbye.

I dragged my suitcase through the living room and down the hall to my private residence. After opening the door fully—I always left it cracked in case Elvira wanted to escape the main house—I glanced around. The sunny yellow comforter hung on the bed with precision, while the yellow and green throw pillows lined up across the headboard like perfect little soldiers. A wooden rocking chair sat in the corner next to the dresser, adjacent to a window. Curling up in the white blanket and sitting in the chair while reading was one of my favorite things to do in the winter, especially when it snowed. Matching yellow curtains kept the room bright and sunny, even during those miserable months.

"Elvira?" I called. "I'm home." Nothing. She was probably hiding under the bed. "When you're done being upset with me, come out. I'd love a good cuddle with you."

After dumping everything in my suitcase into the dirty clothes basket, I returned to the living room and headed up the staircase, noting the banister needed a good oiling and the third stair squeaked. I'd have to call in a someone to fix that.

I pulled some sheets from the hallway closet and hurried into the first bedroom suite. Done in ocean blue, it was my favorite room, besides my own. The previous guests had been neat, and clean-up was over quickly. After scrubbing the bathroom, dusting the dresser, making the bed and vacuuming, I picked up the dirty sheets and towels and glanced around critically, searching for anything out of place. All my reviews online mentioned the cleanliness of my establishment, and I worked hard to maintain that reputation.

"Thank goodness you're finally home," a voice from the hallway called. "Where the heck have you been?"

My spine stiffened and goosebumps prickled over my skin. I knew that voice.

"I know you won't answer me, you never do, but I'm glad to see you. It's been as boring as watching grass grow around here, Bernie. I wish you'd find more interesting friends than that Darla Darling. She's nice and all, but sheesh! What a snoozer she is. Her name certainly doesn't do her justice."

The faint smell of marijuana met my nose as I slowly turned around... and came face-to-face with my dead grandmother.

CHAPTER 2

a scream stuck in my throat as I slapped my hand over my mouth and stared at her standing in the doorway, a purple mumu covering her thin frame. Her long gray hair was parted down the middle and pulled into a ponytail at her nape. "With a name like Darla Darling, you'd think she'd be a stripper or something," she continued. "I do have to admit, the breakfast she brings in looks delicious though. If I could actually eat one of those blueberry muffins, maybe she wouldn't irritate me so much." She narrowed her blue gaze on me. "You can see me, can't you?"

I nodded, then shut my eyes, rubbed them, and opened them again. Still there. My vision became blurry as a buzzing sound sounded from within my head. I dropped the laundry and grabbed the doorframe.

"Woohoo!" my grandma yelled as she danced a little

jig in the hallway. "Finally, someone besides the dang cat knows I'm here!"

Okay, I was having hallucinations. Horrible, terrible hallucinations. Obviously I should have stayed in the hospital a few more days after being hit by lightning. Something in my brain had short-circuited and I was crazy. Certifiable. Completely and utterly bonkers.

I was seeing dead people.

My knees gave out and I sank to the ground as my grandmother, or Ruby, as she liked to be called, continued her dance, her bare feet seeming to float over the carpet.

"What are you doing down there?" she asked. "Get up and let's celebrate! Do you know how long I've gone talking to people and no one answers?"

Perhaps I should call 9-1-1 on myself and request they send me to a psychiatric ward.

She flopped down on the floor in front of me, sitting cross-legged. "What are you doing? Some of that meditation mumbo-jumbo?"

I stared at Ruby, willing her away. "There are no such things as ghosts," I whispered, and she rolled her blue eyes.

"Of course there are, dingbat. I'm sitting right here!"

The apparition looked like my grandma, talked like my grandma, and the faint smell of marijuana and lavender soap lingered in the air, just like it had when she was alive. Yet, I could see right through her to the door on the other side of the hallway.

"Look, I've been stuck in this place for three years

12

with no one to talk to," she continued. "You and I have so much catching up to do!"

My mother, Ruby's daughter, had described her as a 'loose cannon,' a 'troublemaker,' and 'one who lived by her own rules.' I'd also heard 'selfish,' 'horrible mother,' and 'drug addict.' She wasn't the run-of-the-mill grandma. She'd never baked a cookie in her life, so when I visited every summer, we'd have dance parties instead where she'd decorate the living room downstairs in a particular theme. Sometimes it was disco. Other times it was the swinging twenties, or the fifties. She'd pull out trunks of old clothes and we'd dress for the particular era, put on some music, and have our party.

I couldn't recall ever curling up on her lap and reading a book. Instead, I remembered flying through the streets of Sedona and into the mountains on her ATV and holding onto her for dear life as she whooped and hollered. As I got older, she'd pull out the Ouija Board, and swore she was in contact with Frank Sinatra. She let me watch R-rated movies, eat ice cream for breakfast, and stay up past midnight.

She had no idea who my grandfather was, and she never married. So I understood when my mother claimed she played by her own set of rules, because no truer statement had ever been uttered, especially for a woman who grew up in the sixties.

When Ruby had died three years ago while in bed with the handyman, I'd been heartbroken. The woman represented everything in life I would never be, and I found consolation with the fact she'd gone doing something she loved.

"The nice thing about being dead is my joints don't snap and crack when I get up from the floor," she said as she stood.

"This isn't real," I muttered, also rising while grabbing the dirty laundry. "Just ignore it. I need medical help. Go away."

"So tell me where you've been," Ruby said as I walked right through her. "You were gone... what... a week? I tend to lose track of time. Boredom does that to me."

I dropped the soiled sheets in the hallway, grabbed some clean sheets and towels from the closet, and headed to the next bedroom, making sure to tread lightly over the carpet so I didn't disturb my guest. Ruby trailed behind me and never stopped talking.

"You saw me for a second, Bernie. Your face gave that away. Just admit that you're talking to a ghost."

After taking a deep breath, I opened the door to the guestroom that still needed cleaning. They hadn't been nearly as tidy and I groaned in frustration as I surveyed the mess. Beer cans lay on the nightstands and on top of the dresser.

Peals of laughter sounded from behind me. "Oh, wow! I wish I had dropped in on this party!"

I meandered into the bathroom and found my white towels stained with red lipstick. "Who wipes their lipstick off with a towel?" I mumbled while studying the spot and wondering if I'd be able to remove it.

"Someone who had no regard for a good lipstick," Ruby said over my shoulder. "Everyone knows lipstick should be taken off while kissing, not rubbing it on a towel."

Glancing into the mirror, I saw nothing except my own reflection, yet I *felt* her behind me, just as if she were alive. A brief memory of me visiting her during the summer when I was seventeen came to mind. It had been so hot, and we'd decided a day trip to Slide Rock, a natural swimming pool, would be the perfect way to cool off.

When we arrived, Ruby dropped our chairs in the middle of a group of college kids and started up a conversation. Before I knew it, my outgoing grandmother became the center of attention as she flirted with the boys and gave advice to the girls. Someone put a beer in my hand while music started to play. Ruby stripped down to her bikini and yelled, "Dance Party!"

I watched from my chair, wishing I could be as outgoing and social as she was, but it wasn't in my nature. Instead, I tended to be shy and reserved, preferring to watch from the sidelines.

"Your mom is great!" one of the girls said.

With a grin, I nodded and sipped my beer, not bothering to tell her she was actually my grandmother. She'd had my mother early in her twenties and didn't look a day over forty.

I'll never forget the sight of Ruby coming down the

rock slide with a beer in one hand and a joint in the other while screaming in delight.

She'd always encouraged me to live and push boundaries, while my own mother preferred the straight and narrow path. Ruby's behavior that day would have horrified her, and she'd have probably said something to the effect that Ruby needed to act her age.

But back to the ghost and my stained towels.

Dang it.

"I know you know I'm here, Bernie. You keep looking at me. So why aren't you talking to me?"

With a sigh, I grabbed the towels, stripped the bed, and tossed the beer cans into a large trash bag. I even found a few empties under the desk, as well as a spot on the carpet where someone had spilled a beverage. With a curse, I went to get the carpet cleaner and debated whether or not to return their deposit.

"You can't keep ignoring me forever," Ruby said. "I won't let you." I glanced over at her as she stretched out on the bed I'd just made, a huge smile tugging at her mouth, her blue eyes dancing with mischief. "I tried to get your attention for months after you moved in and you never noticed me. I *know* you see me now."

"You aren't real," I said, staring at her. "Go away. You are a product of my injury. I'm going to see a doctor and you'll eventually disappear."

Ruby laughed, a sound that had always made everyone in the room join in. It wasn't a delicate little sound, but an unapologetic loud guffaw that came directly from the gut, and I couldn't help but smile. Admittedly, I was enjoying my brief brush with insanity.

"First, I'll try meditation, to focus my mind," I continued. "If that doesn't work, I'll head to the doctor."

"You aren't going to be able to concentrate me away," Ruby said as she rose from the bed and stood directly in front of me. "And you don't need a doctor, Bernie. I'm dead, and I'm here."

I stared into her eyes and for a brief moment, I believed her. Maybe I wasn't crazy. What if the lightning had opened up some type of connection to the dead? Oh, my gosh. Would I start seeing ghosts wherever I went?

No. I didn't believe in the paranormal. I'd been hit by lightning and something in my brain had short-circuited. That was the only logical excuse. Heck, maybe I just needed some rest.

"I'm finishing up this room, and then I'm going to take a nap. When I get up, you'll be gone."

"You go ahead and believe that, but I'll still be around. You do look tired, though. Did you go on a bender and not invite me?"

"I don't do benders," I muttered as I straightened the pillows on the bed. "I was back in Louisiana for Tilly's wedding."

"How was it?"

I began to tell her about the disaster I'd witnessed,

but then remembered I was talking to my own imagination. "You aren't real," I whispered.

"Okay, you believe what you want," Ruby said with a sigh. "You're absolutely no fun, Bernie."

She strode from the room, leaving behind the scent of marijuana and lavender soap. I stared at the doorway for a long moment and then shook my head. "See? She's gone. A figment of your imagination."

I gathered my cleaning supplies, the dirty linens, and glanced over the room one last time with a critical eye. Much better than when I'd walked in.

After hurrying down the stairs, I started the laundry then went into my own bedroom, falling across the bed. I glanced around the space, which used to be Ruby's, and didn't find any sign of her. Nothing. "Thank goodness," I whispered as I pulled a pillow under my head and curled up on my side.

My cat, Elvira, came out from under the bed and snuggled up next to me. "I'm so happy to see you," I whispered as I stroked her head. "I missed you."

She glanced over at me, then shut her eyes, which seemed like a really good idea, so I followed suit.

I didn't know how long I'd been out when I was jerked awake by Ruby's voice.

"Bernie!" she yelled. "Get up!"

Shooting to my feet, my breath sawed as my hands shook. "What?! What's wrong?!" I found her sitting in my rocking chair. Elvira tore from the room, obviously as upset as I was that our nap had been disturbed.

"Jeez, Bernie. You still sleep like you're dead."

18

"Oh my gosh! Why are you doing this?" I yelled as I grabbed my head. "Why are you hassling me?"

"Don't be such a drama queen," Ruby said. "And I woke you because you need to call the police."

I stared at the ghostly image of my grandmother and wanted to throttle her, but then I realized what she'd said. "Why do I need to call the police?"

"Your guest upstairs? He's a goner."

"What does that mean?" I asked, rubbing my tired eyes. "Are you saying he left already?"

Ruby sighed and shook her head. "He's dead, Bernie."

CHAPTER 3

*H*er statement jolted me out of whatever sleep had been left. My heart thundered as I turned on my heel and ran out of my room and up the stairs. Ruby leaned against the wall next to my guest's room with Elvira standing at her side, staring up at her. I knew at that second my cat could see Ruby and had been watching her since we moved in.

"Okay," I said, standing in front of the door and rubbing my sweaty palms on my jeans. "How do you know he's dead?"

Ruby nodded her head toward the room. "Take a look. It's pretty obvious."

As I laid my hand on the doorknob, I paused for a moment. What if this was part of my hallucination? What if I barged in on my guest and found him sitting on the toilet? What if he then wrote a scathing review about the B&B owner who forced her way in on her customers unannounced?

Knock first.

"What's his name?" I mumbled, shutting my eyes. "Gardner? No that's not it. Gomez?"

"It's Gonzalez. At least that's what I thought I heard when he checked in."

I glanced over at the ghost. "Thanks." Taking a deep breath, I knocked on the door. "Mr. Gonzalez?"

No answer. Crud.

"Mr. Gonzalez?" I called, louder this time. "It's Bernadette Maxwell, the owner. Are you okay?"

Silence.

"He's dead, Bernie," Ruby said as I pressed my ear against the door. "He's not going to answer."

"Are you sure that's his name?"

"Not really, but me remembering his name doesn't make him any less dead."

I swore under my breath and opened the door. Mr. Gonzalez lay on the bed, his eyes open and staring at the ceiling. "Oh, no," I muttered as I walked in.

"See? Deader than Elvis."

I strode over to the side of the bed and gently placed my fingers on his neck. Nothing. His mouth had a strange white foam around it. I stared at him a moment, then the dry heaves overtook me. I raced from the room and back into the hallway. Hands on knees, I took some deep breaths and tried not to throw up.

"Death ain't pretty, Bernie," Ruby said softly from behind me. "Call the police."

She was right. I walked with wooden legs down the

stairs to the living room where I grabbed my phone and dialed. Once I'd reported the body, I sat down and stared at the floor, unable to erase the image of the dead man from my mind.

"Are you okay?"

Glancing over, I found Ruby sitting on the other end of the couch. "How did you find him? Why were you in there?"

"You like to say this place is haunted, so I help you out from time to time," she replied with a shrug. "When I went in there, he didn't look too healthy, and I realized he was a goner."

"You were going in to haunt him?"

"Sure. I haven't got much else to do."

It was then I realized that I was indeed speaking to my dead grandmother, and it didn't seem as upsetting or strange as it had before my nap.

"What exactly are you responsible for around here?" I asked, narrowing my gaze on her. "What do you do to my guests?"

"There isn't a lot I can do, Bernie. Sometimes if I blow on their neck, they'll say they have goosebumps. If I rush at them, they'll mention a cold draft."

Sirens wailed in the distance as I nodded. It was what the customers had reported. I had no idea they were actually experiencing Ruby instead of their own imaginations. "How do you think he died?"

"Don't know. I'm not a doctor, and I didn't play one on television when I was alive. Although, I always thought I'd make a great movie star."

A knock sounded at the front door, and I rose to answer it. Glancing over my shoulder, I noted Ruby remained on the couch, staring at me expectantly with Elvira at her side.

I opened the door to find Deputy Adam Gallagher, and my cheeks immediately flushed. With his blond hair and the bluest eyes I'd ever seen, I'd had a silent crush on him for months. I felt like an insecure, flustered fifteen-year-old-girl instead of a confident thirty-five-year-old woman who owned a business whenever I saw him.

There wasn't any friendly greeting as he pushed past me and our arms brushed against each other, sending a tingle over my skin. "Where's the body?"

"Upstairs. First door on the right."

He nodded and bound up the staircase.

"My goodness, he's a cute one," Ruby said.

"I know."

"Don't date cops, though, Bernie. They're absolutely no fun."

I nodded absently as I sat down again. Adam returned a moment later and took a seat on the couch across from me. Or, I should say, us.

"How're you holding up, Bernie?" he asked as he pulled a pen from his breast pocket and tapped it on the notepad in his hand.

"Okay, I guess," I said. "I'm obviously upset about this."

"Sure you are. Can you tell me what happened?"

"Well, I was taking a nap and—"

23

"Probably not a good idea to mention your dead grandmother woke you," Ruby interrupted. "Makes you look a little bonkers, kiddo. You better pivot and change up the story."

She was right. I cleared my throat, studied my hands for a second and tried to conjure a lie, which I had never excelled at. "I was napping, and when I woke up, I decided to check on my guest and I found him."

"Why did you want to check on him?"

Yes, why indeed. It wasn't like I had ever just randomly barged into another customer's room to see what they had going on.

"Tell him the guest told you an hour ago he had an appointment but wanted to take a nap and needed someone to make sure he was awake," Ruby said.

I repeated her story and Adam stared at me for a moment, his forehead pinched in confusion. "I thought you were napping?"

My hands became sweaty as I tried to continue the lie. "Well... the customer..."

"Oh, for the sake of everything holy, Bernie," Ruby said with a sigh. "You've always been a horrible liar, and it's a skill you need, especially when talking to the police. Trust me on that. Tell him the customer came to you and wanted to be woken in an hour because he didn't have an alarm clock, and you thought a nap sounded like an excellent idea, so you decided to take a snooze as well!"

Once again, I parroted Ruby and that seemed to smooth Adam's puzzlement. He jotted down a few notes on his pad just as Sheriff Bruce Walker strode in. In his seventies, he had a head full of gray hair and a spring in his step. He glanced around before settling his serious gaze on me. I smiled, but he only nodded.

"Hey, Bruce," Adam said.

"Adam. Where's the body?"

"Upstairs. First door on the right."

"I didn't know old Bruce was still around," Ruby said. "He's the reason why I told you not to date cops. That advice comes from personal experience."

Of course, I didn't know much about my grandmother's former dating habits, but her free lifestyle wasn't a good fit for being involved with an officer of the law. Some of her favorite activities were illegal.

The sheriff hurried up the stairs and I returned my attention to Adam. Our gazes locked, and a deep blush once again crawled over my cheeks and down my neck.

Ruby sighed. "You don't want to date a cop, so quit looking at him like he's the best thing since sliced bread, Bernie. The simpering, blushing girl act doesn't suit you."

If only she knew it wasn't an act. The man made my insides feel mushy.

Adam cleared his throat and tapped his pen on his pad once again. Had I noted a tint in his cheeks as well? "So, just to go over this one last time, your customer came downstairs... what's his name?"

"Mr. Gonzalez."

"Right. He came downstairs and said he needed a

nap and wanted you to wake him because he didn't have an alarm clock."

"Correct."

"What about his cell phone?"

I recalled seeing it plugged in, sitting on the bedside table. "He said the battery had gone dead and he was having trouble keeping it charged. He asked me to wake him in case it didn't go off."

"Nice one," Ruby muttered. "Very nice play, my girl."

I smiled and nodded as Adam scribbled in his notebook.

"Then you decided to lay down," he stated, glancing up at me.

"Yes."

"And when you woke, you went upstairs to rouse Mr. Gonzalez, and found him dead."

"Yes."

Wow, it was getting hot in the room. Was it Adam, or all the lies I needed to track?

"Okay. That seems pretty cut and dry. I didn't see any blood or anything."

"Me neither."

We sat in awkward silence for a long moment, then the sheriff came halfway down the stairs. "Adam, can you grab me a crime scene kit out of my car?"

"Sure," the deputy said, shooting to his feet. "Be back in a minute."

Walker turned and hurried back up the stairs.

"What do they need a crime scene kit for?" I whispered, turning to Ruby.

THE GUEST IS A GONER

"Old Bruce must have seen something that convinced him it's a crime scene," she answered.

"Like what?"

"I don't know. Do you want me to go find out?"

"Is that legal? Can you do that?"

Ruby shrugged. "Of course I can go spy on the sheriff, and who cares if it's legal?"

That was my grandmother. Laws didn't pertain to her, even in death.

"Okay, yes! Go!"

My grandmother smiled and disappeared into thin air. Now that I was alone for a brief moment, I had to question my sanity once again. Speaking with Ruby's ghost had proven to be beneficial to me in coming up with a plausible story for the cops. Real or not, I'd take her help as long as she wanted to stick around.

Adam returned and raced up the stairs, blowing right through Ruby as she descended. He stopped mid-stride, grabbed the banister and turned to look at me, his face once again set in a perplexed grimace, then he smiled.

"For a second I thought you were smoking weed," he said with a chuckle. "That's illegal here in Arizona. At least for the time being."

"I'm aware of that, and I don't smoke," I said through gritted teeth. It had become apparent that anytime Ruby was close to someone, they thought they smelled pot.

Adam grinned again and continued up the stairs.

27

"What did you find out?" I whispered as Ruby sat down next to me.

"I'm not sure. Bruce is really interested in the foam around his mouth and was studying the cup next to his bed. I think it said something about smoothies."

"Darla said he checked in while sipping a smoothie from Sarah's Sensational Smoothies."

"I wasn't around much when he came in," Ruby replied. "I only caught bits and pieces and I wasn't paying attention to what was said."

If she wasn't in the house, where did she go?

The sheriff descended the stairs, so the question would have to wait. "I called the EMT to have the body taken to the coroner," he said. "They should be here pretty soon."

I nodded and tried to smile.

He leaned against the mantle and crossed his arms over his chest. "It's my understanding you're Ruby's granddaughter. Is that right?"

"Correct," I replied, shifting in my seat as Ruby began to cackle. Her reputation had always preceded her, and *everyone* knew her. She loved being the bad girl in life, and I'm sure it tickled her to have the sheriff still recalling memories of her, three years after her death. If you hadn't at least heard of her, you had to have been locked away in a basement, or at the very least, didn't get out much.

"I knew her well," he said. "She was a good woman. I was sorry when she died."

"Oh, shut up, you old turd," Ruby scoffed. "You were

praising the day I met my maker. I was too much woman for you."

"Thank you," I replied rather loudly while I tried to talk over the ghost of my grandmother. "I appreciate you saying that."

"Why are you talking so loud?" the sheriff asked. "Are you hard of hearing?"

"No. Yes. Sometimes? I-I don't know."

Ruby continued to laugh, but now I was sure it was directed at me.

"You don't know if you're hard of hearing?" Walker asked.

I shut my eyes and leaned back against the couch, doing my best to ignore the old ghost next to me. "I'm sorry. I'm very tired. I just flew in from my cousin's wedding."

"And how was that?" Walker asked.

Frankly, I didn't have the energy to go into all the details. "It was fine," I lied. It seemed falsehoods came easier and easier by the moment.

Adam came down the stairs as two EMTs wheeled in a gurney. He motioned for them to follow him.

"We're going to have to seal that room off for a day or two, Ms. Maxwell," the sheriff said. "It's a crime scene."

Ruby and I exchanged glances and she furrowed her brow. "What the heck does that mean?"

"Yes," I said. "What does that mean?"

Walker stared at me a moment, as if he were unsure whether all my marbles were lined up nicely. He didn't need to know I'd pondered the same question for most of the day.

"Well, it looks like Mr. Gonzalez was murdered," Walker said. "Most likely poisoned."

My breath caught as I stared at him. Someone had been murdered in my house? By whom?

"Who did it?" Ruby and I asked, in unison.

"Well, we don't know that yet, but for the sake of the investigation, I'd advise you not to wander too far out of town."

CHAPTER 4

"When did you say was the last time you saw him?" Sheriff Walker asked as they wheeled the body outside. Adam followed them and shut the door behind him.

I stared at the closed door, unable to believe the turn my life had just taken.

Ruby said, "You better say something, Bernie, or he's going to put some cuffs on you, and it won't be for a good time, either."

"I-I guess about an hour ago?" I replied, realizing a killer had been in my house. Had I locked the front door when I came home?

"You're sure about that?" Walker asked.

"Y-yes."

The sheriff narrowed his gaze on me. "I'm no expert, but I'd say he's been dead for a few hours, not one."

Great. I'd lied and made this situation so much

31

worse. I shouldn't have listened to Ruby. "It may have been longer than an hour when he came and asked me to wake him," I said. "You know how time flies."

"Actually, I don't. Especially when I'm investigating a murder. Every minute counts."

The room became really warm once again and the walls seemed to be closing in around me. "Would you like some water?" I asked, my voice coming out a little squeaky. "I could use some."

"You're so uptight right now, I'd suggest a shot of tequila," Ruby said.

"No thanks," Walker said. "Why don't you fetch some water and come back in here so we can continue our conversation?"

"Of course," I mumbled as I rose from the couch. I motioned for Ruby to follow me and I didn't meet the sheriff's gaze as I marched into the kitchen.

While I pulled a glass from the cabinet and filled it, Ruby appeared next to me. I startled and dropped it into the sink with a crash. Shards of glass scattered all across the basin.

"Everything okay in there?" Walker called.

"Yes! I'm just a little clumsy!" I yelled, then turned to Ruby. "Don't sneak up on me like that!"

"I didn't, Bernie. You're wound tighter than a girdle at a pancake breakfast. You need to relax!"

"I lied to the police and he's caught me in that lie," I hissed. "There's a murder investigation going on, in case you missed that part." Tears welled in my eyes. "Oh, my word. I've lied during a murder investigation."

Ruby waved her hand in front of her face. "Not a big deal. I'm sure it happens all the time."

I shook my head and retrieved another glass. After filling it, I downed the liquid in one long gulp. My hands shook and my breathing came in short spurts.

"Seriously, Bernie. You need to calm down. You're going to give yourself an ulcer."

"This is what I do when I'm stressed, or worried, or being confronted by an officer of the law during a murder investigation. I panic."

"Well, panicking isn't going to do anything for you except give you wrinkles. Get another glass of water, take some deep breaths, and come back out to the living room."

I stood at the sink and did as I was told, feeling mildly better. Returning to the living room, I grinned at the sheriff as I sat down.

"Getting back to our conversation, you sure you talked to him an hour ago, or do you want to amend your statement?"

My thoughts flew to the day's events. Mr. Gonzalez was already checked in when I arrived home. Darla had done the honors. We chatted for a bit then I cleaned the rooms, met Ruby, and took a nap.

No one had been in my house except me... well, that I was aware of, anyway. Oh, heck—was I now a suspect?

"It may have been earlier today," I said. "I've been so busy trying to catch up from my trip. I honestly wasn't watching the clock all that well."

The sheriff stared at me for a long moment, and I tried not to wilt under his gaze. Finally, he said, "Okay. I'll be in touch soon. And remember, don't go into the room until we clear it."

"How long will that be?"

"Maybe a couple of days."

I nodded and walked him to the front door. "Thanks for coming," I said. "I appreciate it."

He waved over his shoulder as he strode down the walkway. I shut the door, locked it, turned around, and sank to the floor, placing my forehead on my knees.

I had to order my thoughts. The sheriff obviously believed something hinky had happened because my story had changed. Then there was the fact that I was the only one in the house most of the day, which cast suspicion on me as the murderer.

"Get up and let's have a dance party for old times' sake!" Ruby said cheerfully, twirling in a circle in front of me.

"I don't want to dance," I grumbled, standing. "I might be in big trouble here!"

Ruby rolled her eyes and crossed her arms over her chest. "Why on earth do you think that?"

"Because I was the only one here today!" I yelled. "What if they think I killed him?"

"What if they do? Don't they need little minor details called evidence? There isn't any."

Evidence. In the crime shows, they looked for things like murder weapons and fingerprints. I'd touched the doorknob, so fingerprints there. Inside the room, they'd probably find a couple of mine, and definitely others. I cleaned fanatically but was it enough to actually erase fingerprints? I had no idea.

Since the sheriff had said he thought Mr. Gonzalez had been poisoned, I wondered what type had been used. My knowledge of poisons was limited, except the obvious things like don't eat laundry detergent or drink Draino. Did I have whatever had been used hanging around my house? Wouldn't someone taste it if they drank lighter fluid or insect killer and immediately spit it out?

I ran to my cleaning supply closet and threw open the doors. Pulling out one canister after the other, I read the warning labels. Gosh dang it. I had at least a dozen bottles labeled as poison.

"What are you looking for?" Ruby asked from behind me.

And a ghost. I had a ghost as well.

I shut the door and sighed. "I was seeing what I had that could poison someone."

"And?"

"There's a lot."

I returned to the living room and plopped down on the couch. Ruby appeared next to me. Poor Mr. Gonzalez. I'd never spoken to the man, but guilt wracked my insides. He'd died in my house.

"You know, he could have committed suicide as well," Ruby said. "Maybe it's not murder at all. Perhaps he sucked down a bottle of bleach."

A knock sounded at the front door and I glanced

over at it, debating whether to answer or not. For all I knew, the sheriff had come to drag me to prison.

"You better see who it is," Ruby said. "It could be your guests who made reservations earlier. Remember?"

Right.

The last thing I wanted to do was smile and pretend I was happy to see total strangers. What if they ended up dead as well?

What if a ghost was responsible for killing Mr. Gonzalez? She and I had been the only ones in the house during the murder, and I certainly hadn't kill the man.

I turned to Ruby and realized I knew next to nothing about her... current state. What was she capable of? Disappearing into thin air - check. Ghosting through walls and people - check. Murder? Hmm...

My grandmother, while alive, may have been a wild child until the day she died, but she'd never intentionally hurt someone. Or did something short-circuit in her brain when she passed that turned her into a killer? Maybe it was a deep-seated fantasy of hers that she now fulfilled in death, where she couldn't get caught and no one would suspect her?

The knock sounded again. "You and I need to have a talk after these people check in," I muttered. Unbelievable. I thought chatting with a ghost was no longer a big deal.

"Can't wait!" Ruby called as I walked to the door.

"Welcome!" I said as I opened the panel and was met with a couple pulling suitcases behind them instead of the sheriff dangling handcuffs from his fingers. "My name's Bernadette, but please, call me Bernie."

"We're the Thompsons," the man said, holding his hand out. "I'm Bob, and she's Bobbie. We're so glad to be here!"

The cuteness turned my stomach, but I laid my palm in his for a brief moment, then motioned for them to follow me inside. When I'd first opened the B&B, I'd set up a little check-in desk in the corner and it functioned well. It didn't take away from the beauty of the room, but I had a central place to store keys, the credit card machine, and brochures belonging to the other businesses in town.

I pegged my customers in their early thirties, maybe late twenties. They seemed nice enough.

I glanced over at Ruby as I got the Thompsons checked in. She had sprawled out on the couch with her arm thrown over her forehead as if my guests bored her to tears.

The Thompsons, however, oohed and aahed over the living room. I had to admit, it was stunning with the high ceilings, ornate wood molding, and large fireplace.

"Is this place really haunted?" Bobbie asked.

Before, I would have smiled and nodded conspiratorially, but not today as I watched Ruby float up from the couch and walk toward us with her hands stretched out in front of her like a zombie while she moaned and groaned. When she got right behind my guests, she shouted, "Boo!"

"Different people have different experiences," I said.

"We're hoping we see a ghost," Bob said. "We love stuff like that."

"Well, with any luck, you will," I replied as Ruby turned in a circle, waving her hands above her head while making "ooooh" noises. Unfortunately, she didn't resemble scary in the least bit.

"Let's get you up to your room," I said, pursing my lips together so I didn't laugh. My grandmother may be the worst haunter I'd ever witnessed. Not that I'd ever seen a ghost before. But if other ghosts were as bad at their jobs as she was, the scariness of the paranormal world had been highly overrated.

I led them up the stairs and cringed when I noted the yellow police tape on the door to my right. It went right across from one doorjamb to the other and read *Police: do not enter.* I noted they'd also placed a strip directly on the door itself. In order to get into the room, I'd have to break the seal, and they'd know I'd entered.

"What happened there?" Bob asked as I stuck my key into the door to their room.

"Nothing," I said, smiling. "I'm having some work done in there and it's not safe. I just want to make sure my guests avoid the room."

Bobbie laughed. "For a second I thought it was a murder scene or something like that!"

I chuckled right along with her. "Nothing that exciting, I'm afraid." I handed the key to her and motioned for them to enter. I convinced myself I hadn't lied. The sheriff had said he thought Gonzalez had been poisoned, but he couldn't rule it a murder just yet. "Breakfast will be tomorrow at eight. For dinner, I highly recommend Darling's Diner, and if you're interested in seeing Sedona and the surrounding area, Jumping Jack's Jeep Tours is the way to go."

"Oh! I wanted to do that!" Bobbie exclaimed.

"You'll find a brochure in your room so you can make your reservations," I said, pointing to the desk next to the bed.

"Thanks," Bob said. "We'll drop our bags and head out in a bit. We're actually renting bikes for the rest of the afternoon."

"Have a great time!"

"You forgot about sunset yoga," Ruby said, materializing behind them.

I nodded and walked down the hallway, not possessing the frame of mind for yoga. Stress and being a potential murder suspect didn't gel with Cobra or Warrior pose, although, it was probably exactly what I should be doing to lower my anxiety.

"They're going to be busy, and so am I," I muttered as I hurried downstairs with Ruby trailing me. "Get into my room now, please."

My ghost and I were going to have a long chat. I'd find out exactly why she was here and what she could do to help me get out of my current predicament.

CHAPTER 5

J shut the door to my bedroom—which used to be Ruby's—and turned around, expecting to see her lounging on the bed. Instead, the room was empty. With a huff, I sat in the rocking chair and waited for her to make an appearance.

Two minutes later, she floated through the door as if she didn't have a care in the world... or a grand-daughter on the verge of a nervous breakdown. "You took your time," I said. "We may not have a lot of it to waste."

"Oh, my gosh. Please quit with the dramatics."

"A man died in this house today, and the sheriff thinks it might be murder."

"And it might be suicide," Ruby said as she lay down across the foot of the bed. "Start worrying about things when you have something to worry about, Bernie."

"No. I want to be prepared. I could go to prison! I was the only one in the house all day!"

"That's not true. That boring girl, Darla, was here. She could have offed him."

"Darla isn't a killer," I replied. "She doesn't have a mean bone in her body."

Ruby muttered something about Darla sucking the fun out of every room and could therefore suck the soul out of a living human, but I didn't ask for clarification. Talk about dramatics.

She sighed and stared at me, obviously not sharing my near hysteria. "So what's this powwow about?"

I took a deep breath and tried to arrange my thoughts into some type of order, but it was futile. There were so many unanswered questions having to do not only with the dead guy, but with Ruby and me. I decided to start from square one. "Why are you here?"

Ruby's brow furrowed in confusion. "Because you asked me into the room!"

"No. That's not what I meant. You died three years ago. Why are you here? Why haven't you... moved on? Gone to heaven? Or is haunting your own house as good as it gets?"

"Ah, I see. To answer your question, I don't know. One minute I'm in bed with the handyman and I'd just gotten up to put on my mumu and I lit a Mary Jane. The next minute, I'm floating toward a blinding light brighter than the sun. The whole experience was pretty shocking, so I didn't really hear what was being said to me, but then I was sucked back into the house and the handyman was about to have a nervous breakdown. I quickly realized no one could see me and I'd kicked the bucket. The ambulance showed up, along with that cute EMT that tried to revive me... oh, man, what a mess. That's the short version. That EMT tried to slip me the tongue, though."

"He did not!" I yelled. "You were dead, and that's just gross! Can we please keep this conversation on track?"

"Shh," Ruby said with a giggle. "They'll hear you upstairs. And I'm kidding about the EMT. I wish he had, though, because he was really a looker. Hotter than even James Dean."

Shutting my eyes, I rubbed my temples with my forefingers. "Ruby, please..."

"Oh, fine," she said with a huff. "What else do you want to know?"

"Can you leave?"

Ruby snorted. "Believe me, I've tried. I can't go beyond the house, but I can go into this weird space that has that bright light. It's like a tunnel, except there isn't any traffic. Very peaceful though. I spend some time there when things get too boring around here, which, I'm sad to say, is quite often."

I ignored the jab.

"And you've been haunting my guests?"

"Well, as much as I'm capable," Ruby replied. "I'm a terrible ghost."

At least we agreed on that.

"Why did you turn this house into a B&B?" Ruby asked. "I left it for you so you could have a place of your own that you love."

I did adore Sedona—the people, the scenery, the weather... I loved everything about it and I had been thrilled to learn Ruby had left her house to me. But what I had discovered upon moving here permanently from Louisiana was that I needed a much bigger income than working at the Sedona dollar store and teaching a few yoga classes in order to keep the house and myself afloat. "I couldn't afford it if I didn't. I needed a way to generate income, and the empty bedroom suites seemed to be the best way."

Ruby nodded. "Touché. It's a big place, and it's getting old. It's an expensive house."

While alive, Ruby had supported herself as a psychic. For a while, she'd even had her own hotline for people to call in and she'd quickly reached a low level of celebrity status. People would come from all over the world to get a reading from her, and she had set hours for her phone calls. I never knew how much money she'd made, but based on the house I now lived in, which was paid for, she'd done quite well.

As I stared at my grandmother, emotion overtook my anxiety while memories flooded in from our time together. I'd come every summer from the time I was ten until I turned seventeen. After that, I'd had responsibilities like jobs and I'd wanted to spend time with friends. Ruby had been placed on the backburner, and guilt washed through me that I'd gone over a decade without seeing her, and then she died.

"Why in the world are you crying?" she asked.

"I'm... I'm just so glad to see you," I whispered. "I'm sorry I was such a horrible granddaughter."

"Oh, knock It off," Ruby said, sitting up. "You had your own life and your mother chattering in your ear, and that's okay. Can we get back to the critical questions at hand?"

I wasn't really sure what she meant by the jab at my mom, but I let it slide. We had more important things to discuss. "Like who committed the murder, if there really was one?" I asked, blowing my nose.

"Well, there is that, but I was wondering why you can see me. Why now? I spent months trying to get your attention when you first arrived and finally gave up. And now, you return from some wedding and we're sitting here having a chat. What happened?"

I found it both endearing and unsettling that Ruby was more interested in discovering what had happened to me than the dead guy who had been upstairs.

And frankly, I didn't know why I could suddenly see Ruby, but I had an idea. Only one strange and significant thing had taken place.

"My cousin, Tilly, invited me out to her wedding," I began. "It was a disaster. An alligator showed up during their vows and someone was murdered. I went to a Voodoo ceremony to help release the spirit of the victim who was trapped on this side."

"Oh! A Voodoo ceremony! How intriguing! I've never been to one!"

Maybe I could do something like that for Ruby? Release her spirit from this plane to the next? It was a far-fetched idea. This was Sedona. We had our fair share of quirky people, but no Voodoo priestesses I was aware of.

"Yes, it was interesting. I also got hit by lightning."

Ruby clucked her tongue and sat up. "You get zapped and you can see me. Interesting."

To put it mildly.

"Hate to say this, but I'm glad you got hit," Ruby said. "It's nice to be seen, especially by my favorite granddaughter. I'm glad you weren't badly hurt."

I didn't bother to point out I was her only grand-daughter, and I appreciated her situation, but my anxiety still shot through the roof over the dead man.

"Can we get back to Mr. Gonzalez?"

"Sure, honey. What about him?"

I tried to recall if the police had taken anything out of the room, besides the body, and in my panic of being caught in a lie, I couldn't. "Can you go into that room and do an inventory of what you see now, compared to what you found when you discovered him?"

"Sure. I guess so," Ruby replied with a shrug.

"Okay, great. Can you look for a suicide note? Perhaps some indication that he killed himself?"

I hated that the man had died, but if he'd done himself in, it would be a relief. At least I wouldn't be wondering if I'd had a murderer in my house while I slept.

"Why don't you just go in and poke around yourself?"

"Because the police asked me not to. Besides, they

taped up the door. If I break the seal, they'll know I've been in there contaminating their crime scene."

Ruby rolled her eyes. "It's your house. You can do what you want."

"I'm going to do what they asked me to," I said, trying to keep the irritation out of my voice.

"Fine. I'll go take a look. Do you want me to check in on the Thompsons as well?"

I shook my head. "Let's just concentrate on Mr. Gonzalez for now."

"They were hoping for a run in with a ghost," Ruby said, waving her hands above her head again. "You shouldn't disappoint your customers."

"Mr. Gonzalez for right now," I said, standing and beginning to pace. "We'll worry about haunting the Thompsons later."

Ruby slipped through the door while I chewed my nails. The police should have let me know if they'd found a suicide note, but I hoped that maybe it had fallen under the bed or something.

And frankly, I worried that Mr. Gonzalez had been trapped on this plane, like Ruby. I didn't think I could handle living with two ghosts.

After a few moments, she returned.

"What did you find?"

"Nothing exciting," she replied with a shrug. "Body is gone, but they also took the cup from the smoothie place from the nightstand. I didn't see his little overnight bag he came in with. Honestly, he didn't arrive with much, now that I think about it."

"Did you search in the closet? Check the dresser drawers?"

"Can't do that, honey," Ruby said. "I'm dead, remember? I can't move inanimate objects. If I could, this whole haunting gig would be a lot more fun."

I nodded, supposing she was right. Frankly, if my stuff had started floating around the house, I would have put it up for sale in a heartbeat.

"You should check his car, though," Ruby said.

Of course I should. It never occurred to me to question how he'd arrived at my doorstep, and apparently, the police hadn't considered it either.

"Where is it?" I asked.

"Out back. That black beater that should have been taken to scrap years ago."

I rushed over to my bed and stood on it, then opened the blinds to the window above it. A little black Honda that had definitely seen better days had been parked in the lot behind the house, right next to my SUV. I never would have paid any attention to it. People parked back there all the time—tourists as well as locals who couldn't find any other parking on the roads. It was a busy lot, especially since there weren't any fees to use it.

"We don't have keys," I mumbled. "I don't know how to break in."

Ruby joined me on top of the bed, and we both stared out the window. "That's something that should be taught in high school along with changing a tire and how to swap out a lightbulb and balance a checkbook."

"No one below the age of forty has a checkbook any longer, Ruby. It's all done online."

"And that's the problem. People swipe the card and don't realize how much they're spending. The state of people your age is pathetic. So much debt, not enough joy, and too much anxiety medicine."

I couldn't argue. At thirty-five, I ticked off a lot of those boxes, as did everyone I knew. At least I tried to manage my anxiety through healthy eating and yoga, which seemed to be failing me today in an epic fashion.

"Go take a gander," Ruby whispered. "There may be something in there that tells us whether he was murdered or committed suicide."

"Like what?"

"I don't know! Go look!"

After stepping off the bed, I slipped on my sneakers and hurried outside.

The dirt lot that sat behind my house wasn't surrounded by much except a couple other houses to my left and some desert and mountains to my right. As I strode to the vehicle, I couldn't squash the feeling someone was watching me, which was ridiculous.

I glanced in through the car window, then back at the doorway where Ruby stood, looking so forlorn I almost felt sorry for her. As someone who tended to be a homebody, I didn't fully appreciate her need to be out and about. But if I turned it around and thought of myself as never being home, well, then I completely understood.

My phone rang and I about jumped out of my skin.

I didn't answer when I didn't recognize the number. It quickly rang again.

"Hello?"

"Stay away from the car," a mechanical voice said. "Step away from it."

My heart leapt into my throat as I slowly turned in a circle. Someone *was* watching me. I looked over at the houses and squinted to see inside the windows facing me. Unfortunately, the sun reflected off them perfectly and I couldn't make out anyone.

"Listen very carefully," the voice said. "You don't go near the car. You don't tell the police about this phone call. If you don't do as I tell you, you'll end up just like José Gonzalez, except your death won't be as pleasant."

CHAPTER 6

*O*h. *My. Goodness.*

I stared at my screen, unable to move. My breath came in short spurts while my hands began to tremble.

"What's wrong?"

Glancing up, I found Ruby standing in front of me. I could see straight through her to the open back door. But wait, she couldn't leave the house. This only added to my confusion and I once again questioned my own sanity. I'd done that too many times for one day.

"What... what are you doing?" I asked, looking around again.

"I saw you were upset, so I came to find out what was wrong," Ruby replied, her brow pinched in worry.

"But you said you couldn't leave the house."

"Apparently, I can. It must be something to do with you. You can see me, and maybe with you I can... we're somehow tied together? It doesn't matter. You're so pale, you look like you've seen another ghost. What was the call about, Bernie?"

I glanced around again and headed for the house. Whoever watched me would notice me talking to myself, and I didn't need them thinking I was crazy on top of scared. Crazy, frightened people did desperate things, and I wanted to assure them that I wasn't one of those. That I didn't need to meet the same fate as José Gonzalez.

Huh. Didn't know his name was José.

I shut the door behind us and leaned up against the panel, closing my eyes for a moment. Ruby stood directly in front of me, staring at me expectantly.

"They told me to stay away from the car and not to tell the police about the call," I said. "If I didn't, I'd meet the same fate as Mr. Gonzalez, whose first name is José."

"Interesting," Ruby replied, crossing her arms over her chest. "So someone was watching you."

I nodded.

"What's in that car?" Ruby muttered as she began to pace the kitchen.

"We need to go to the police," I said. "I should call Sheriff Walker right now and tell him—"

"Absolutely not," Ruby said, shaking her head. "They're spying on you. Whatever this mess is, we can be certain of that."

"We also discovered Mr. Gonzalez was murdered."

"You're right. We've found ourselves right in the middle of a big, rotten, smelly pickle."

Footsteps sounded upstairs, and I decided I needed to return to my bedroom to continue my conversation with Ruby there. If my guests overheard me, they'd think I was nuts, which very well could be true, but they didn't need to know that. "Come on," I whispered, motioning for my ghost to follow me. We slipped into my bedroom and I gently shut the door. Hopefully, the Thompsons would be on their way soon and I'd be free to move about the house and talk to her without worry.

She lounged on my bed once again, this time staring up at the ceiling. Elvira came out from under the mattress and settled on the pillows next to Ruby. I was beginning to think my cat liked my ghost better than me.

"So, what do we do?" I asked. "Pretend nothing ever happened?"

"Of course not," she said, shaking her head.

"I should go to the police."

"Oh, heck no. You heard the threat. They're watching you, Bernie. They'll know the second you do."

"Then what's my plan?" I asked as tears welled in my eyes. Plopping down in my rocking chair, I realized that my life was in danger and I had turned to a ghost that may or may not exist to help me figure out what to do about it.

"First off, go get yourself a glass of wine," Ruby said. "Your anxiety is like a palpable force in this room. You're making *me* anxious."

"It's three o'clock in the afternoon."

"Just go grab a bottle. It's five o'clock somewhere."

I listened with my ear against the door before exiting my room. After slipping into the kitchen, I could hear the Thompsons still upstairs. I poured myself a glass, took a sip, then grabbed the bottle and headed back to Ruby.

She eyed me as I sat down in my rocking chair and drank my wine. "I wish I wasn't dead," she said with a sigh. "I sure miss tequila shots."

A giggle escaped me as the wine seeped through my brain. She had been right—I actually did feel a little bit better.

"Now that you're acting like a human again, let's figure this out," Ruby said, sitting up. "There's obviously something in that car that no one wants you to see."

"Agreed."

"In fact, they'd be happy to kill you if you do find it."

My stomach flipped, so I drank more wine. "Yes."

"I'm thinking it's drugs."

Taking another sip from my glass, I furrowed my brow. "Why in the world would you think that?"

"Well, there are a few reasons. First, people die all the time over drugs. Happens in every city, every day."

"Okay, but this is Sedona. We aren't in New York or Los Angeles."

"For all you know, you've stumbled on the biggest drug ring Arizona has ever seen."

Sedona was located off the highway that cut

through the state to the north, which broke off to the east and the west.

"Besides, it's a pretty drive. I bet even drug dealers like nice scenery," Ruby continued. "Once they get to Flagstaff, they have the option of heading toward California or driving over to New Mexico. My guess is old José came in through Tucson and stopped here for the night."

"And someone killed him. But why?"

"Who knows?" Ruby said. "Like I mentioned before, maybe you've got yourself tied up with a big drug organization. They kill for any reason. I used to watch documentaries on the Mexican cartels. Those are some really bad people."

"What do I do now, then?" I asked, once again near tears. The talk of cartels scared the heck out of me. I'd seen the same documentaries showcasing the horrors they were capable of.

"You need to find out who murdered José," Ruby said with a shrug. "You need to pop the lid off this case and solve it."

I had to be going crazy. There was no other option for my mental state and the things this possible figment of my imagination was saying to me. And the fact I was answering her. "How exactly do I go about doing that?"

"You got me there." Ruby stretched out on the bed again. "I've never had to investigate a killing before, but let me tell you, I'm here for this one. It's about time something exciting happened around here."

I turned and stared out the window, trying to come up with a plan. If I could find the murderer, I would be safe. If I phoned the police, the caller had made it very clear I'd meet my demise.

"Was it a man or woman who phoned?" Ruby asked.

"Beats me," I replied. "It was a mechanical voice. Like a robot or something."

"Okay, well, we know it could be either a man or a woman. We're off to a good start on solving the murder."

I knew she was trying to be funny, but it did nothing to lighten the heaviness in my chest.

With a sigh, I had no idea what to do next but drink more wine. We sat in silence for a long while, then a thought hit me like a... well, like a proverbial lightning strike. I'd already been through the real thing, and this was a bit different.

"I'm calling my cousin, Tilly," I said as I grabbed my phone off the dresser and scrolled through my address book. "She's actually solved a couple of murders in her hometown in California. I bet she'll know what to do."

Ruby stared at me as the phone rang, and I was going to set it to speaker, but I heard the Thompsons downstairs. Dang it. *Leave!*

"Bernie!" Tilly answered. "How are you? Where are you?"

"I'm back at home," I said, trying to keep my voice quiet.

"What's wrong?" she asked. "Are you feeling okay?"

It was now or never. I had to confide in someone

and tell them what was happening to me. Tilly and I had been close growing up, and I trusted her. I'd had a great time at her wedding until I'd been hit by lightning. In my gut, I knew I'd made the right phone call.

After taking a deep breath, I blurted, "I feel fine but something weird is happening."

"What's that?"

"Well, I'm not sure how to put this, so I'm just going to say it and hope you don't think I'm insane."

"Okay," she said. "Tell me."

"Tilly, since I was hit by lightning, I'm seeing ghosts."

"You're seeing... ghosts?"

"Yes. Well, one particular ghost. My grandmother, Ruby."

Tilly was silent for a moment, and I thought she'd hung up on me. I wouldn't have blamed her. "Crazy Ruby?" she finally asked.

"Yes."

"She's been dead... what, three or four years?"

I glanced over at my grandmother and drank another sip of wine. "Yes. Three years."

"Have you been to the doctor, Bernie?"

"No. But listen to me. That's the least of my worries right now. She's actually being quite helpful."

"You have more to worry about than a ghost?"

"Yes. I need to solve a murder, and I don't have any idea where to start. You said you've found a couple of killers. What do I do?"

"Why do you have to solve a murder?"

"I'm afraid that if I don't, I'm going to end up dead. Ruby thinks we may be dealing with a drug cartel."

"Are you kidding me?" Tilly shrieked.

"No. What do I do?"

"Oh, my word," Tilly mumbled. "Go to the police."

"Let's pretend that's not an option," I said with a huff.

"It should be an option, Bernie. Those people are insane. Have you seen any of those documentaries?"

Apparently, a lot of people sat through the gruesome television shows. Tilly had always been pretty level-headed, so I found a bit of solace knowing it just wasn't me and Ruby.

"Yes. And this is important, so can we please get back to my question?"

Tilly sighed and she may have cursed a bit, but it was muffled and I couldn't fully hear it. "The way I solved my murders was to talk to people. Look for clues that led me to others that led me to the killer."

"Okay, I can do that."

"Who died, Bernie?"

"A customer of mine."

"When did you find him?"

"I didn't. Ruby did. She came and got me. I lied to the police about it."

"Why did you lie to them?"

"Because my ghost told me to. I wasn't thinking clearly at the time."

"Therefore, the police may think you had something to do with it," Tilly said with a sigh. "I don't know what's more disturbing though: you're seeing ghosts, you may be involved with a cartel, or you lied to the police."

"Yes. It's quite the pot of... stuff."

"Okay, start with everyone you know he came in contact with," Tilly said. "Who checked him in? Was he anywhere in town before?"

"Got it," I said, feeling better now that I had a bit of a plan. "Thanks, Tilly."

"Bernie?"

"Yes?"

"Please go see a doctor."

I glanced over at Ruby who grinned, floated up the ceiling until her nose touched it, then back down where she once again rested against the mattress. I wanted to think of her as my angel, but she was definitely the devil in disguise, and always had been.

But that's why I'd loved her when she'd been alive, and why I was so grateful for her now.

There wasn't any time to seek medical care for my hallucinations or my appreciation of them.

My ghost, whether real or an incredible figment of my imagination, had been the only one to stand by me in these horribly trying times the past few hours. If she was real, she was on my side. If not, well, she was still on my team, and my mind had conjured her for a reason. I'd keep going with her until she either disappeared or no longer steered me right.

Ruby and I had a murder to solve.

CHAPTER 7

*D*arla arrived the next morning promptly at seven with breakfast. I greeted her at the back door and noted the black Honda still sat exactly where it had previously been, seemingly untouched. I glanced around searching for anyone suspicious but found no one that fit the bill.

"Just two this morning?" she asked as we ladled the eggs into a bowl.

"Yes. The Thompsons." I had yet to tell her about Mr. Gonzalez and she obviously hadn't read the local news quite yet. "I guess you didn't hear what happened yesterday?"

"No," she said, setting the croissants out on a white plate.

"Mr. Gonzales was found dead upstairs."

Her eyes almost bugged out of her head as her tongs clanged to the floor. "What?"

"You heard me."

"Oh... oh my gosh. What happened? How?"

"Remember, you can't tell her it's a murder," Ruby said from behind me. "You aren't supposed to know that for sure—only the people who killed him."

"We aren't sure," I said, appreciating Ruby's reminder. The big M Word had been on the tip of my tongue. "The sheriff seems to think he was poisoned."

Which, in all honesty, was saying the same thing as he was murdered, unless he imbibed a bleach cocktail by himself. According to my caller, that hadn't been the case.

Darla ran her hand through her hair, then bent over to retrieve the tongs. "Oh, wow. I'm so sorry to hear that, Bernie. He seemed like a nice guy. Who would want to poison him?"

"I'm not sure," I replied. "Did you notice anything strange about him? Anything that seemed out of sorts?"

She shook her head, but then the proverbial light-bulb went off as she remembered something and her face lit up.

"Bingo!" Ruby called. "Darling Darla has a thought!"

I turned and grimaced at my grandmother. It was obvious she didn't like Darla all that much, but if she didn't have anything nice to say, she should keep her mouth shut.

"He got into a fight before he came in with Stan from As the Pins Drop," Darla said. "I thought I heard loud voices so I glanced out the front window. They were standing on the walkway arguing about something."

Okay, good. We were getting somewhere with my investigation. As the Pins Drop was the local bowling alley, of which Stan was the owner. "What did they say?"

"I'm not sure, Bernie. I couldn't really hear any words, and you know I don't like to stick my nose into other people's business."

"Of course she doesn't," Ruby chimed in. "If she did, her life might be a little more interesting."

"What happened after the argument?" I asked. "Did they hit each other? Who walked away first?"

"Definitely Mr. Gonzalez," Darla said. "He wanted no part of Stan."

"Did he mention anything when he came in?"

She shrugged and shook her head. "Like what?"

"I don't know. What did he say?"

"That he was tired and really wanted to lie down. He'd been driving all day."

"Well there you go," Ruby said. "That fits my drug dealer theory that he drove up from Tucson. This case is almost solved."

"I wonder what he and Stan fought about," I mused.

"You could ask Stan about that," Ruby said. "He's an okay guy. A bit of a bully, but not scary."

"I don't know, but I'm going to take off," Darla said, giving me a hug. "Do you want to go for a run later?"

"Thanks, but no. I've got a lot to do around here." Like solve a murder.

Just then, the Thompsons came down the stairs. Thankfully, they'd arrived from their exploring fairly early last night and apparently had intentions of starting their day early, which fit in with my murder-solving schedule.

"Good morning!" I said as they came into view.

"Good morning!" they replied in unison as they sat down. I noted they had on hiking boots, so I expected they'd be gone a few hours.

"This looks lovely!" Bobbie said. "Is there any coffee?"

"Of course. Let me grab some for you."

I returned to the dining room a moment later with two steaming mugs and some cream and sugar on a silver platter. "Can I get you anything else? Ketchup? Salt and pepper?"

"No, thanks," Bobbie said.

"Did you sleep well?" I asked.

Ruby burst out laughing and I slid my gaze over to her. She danced in circles behind them while Elvira perched on the couch, watching her with curiosity.

"Well, actually, I think we may have had an encounter with your ghost."

I folded my arms over my chest. "Oh, really? What happened?"

"Just blasts of cold air throughout the night," Bob said. "It was a bit creepy, but thankfully, they didn't last long."

"We found a blanket in the closet, so we survived," Bobbie said with a shrug. "It's why we chose this place. We wanted to have a paranormal experience while we're here."

If they could see my big spooky ghost dressed in a purple mumu twirling behind them, I was certain they'd feel cheated.

"What are your plans today?" I asked, changing the conversation.

"We're heading to one of the vortexes to meditate and get in a quick yoga practice," Bob said. "Then do some hiking."

"Which vortex?"

"Probably the Cathedral Rock. We're planning to make it a day trip."

"I can provide you with some bottled water, which you'll definitely need," I offered.

"That would be great. Thank you!"

"That's an excellent place to meditate," I said. "Would you like more information on Cathedral Rock, or do you feel pretty educated on it?"

Bobbie shook her head as she buttered her croissant. "No. Please, tell us more."

I explained Cathedral Rock was a magnetic vortex full of yin, or feminine energy. "It's a very soft, nurturing flow of energy that enhances your meditation practices. But with all vortexes, it also augments your moods. If you're feeling happy, you'll experience bliss. If you're a bit on the cranky side, you may get incredibly irritated." I gave them a wink. "Make sure you're in a good mood before you go, and watch your thoughts while you're there."

"What about the Bell Rock vortex?" Bobbie asked.

"That's more of a masculine energy," I replied. "An

electric vortex is a great place to get your chi moving through you—like a hard yoga flow or some serious chanting."

"You should tell them it's also a great place for tequila shots," Ruby chimed in. "The chanting is so much more effective after tequila."

I ignored her and chatted with the Thompsons until they had finished their breakfast. Once they left, I cleaned up the table and started in on the dishes. With breakfast over and my guests out of the house, I looked for Ruby, who was nowhere to be found.

"Ruby?"

I found Elvira napping on the couch. Apparently, Ruby had disappeared for a while. Maybe she'd gone to her tunnel she'd mentioned—the peaceful place. After taking a seat next to Elvira, I glanced around the big living room and sighed. The house felt empty without Ruby's constant chatter and dancing. Surprisingly, I missed her company and a small chill of fear traveled over me. I also felt safer with her around, which was ridiculous since I was the only one who could see her, besides my cat.

"I'm sure she'll be back," I whispered, stroking Elvira's head.

Until then, I had things to do.

First and foremost, I wanted to talk to Stan at As the Pins Drop and see why he was arguing with Mr. Gonzalez. Second, the police had shown great interest in the smoothie cup, so I should probably go speak to

Sarah. But I had no idea what to ask her besides whether she'd poisoned the man.

Third, I wondered if there was a way for me to get into that car and find out exactly what was in there. If I knew what they'd hidden in it, maybe it would give me some clue as to who the killer was. However, on the flipside of that, if Ruby had been correct and it was drugs, I didn't want to tangle with a cartel.

"Boo!"

I sprang from the couch and whipped around to find Ruby in a fit of giggles. "I've been doing that for three years and it's so much fun to finally get a reaction from you. Even Elvira doesn't move anymore!"

"Don't do that again!" I yelled as she walked around the sofa and sat down. "You scared me to death!"

"Okay, party pooper. I'm sorry. Come sit with your old grandma."

I took a deep breath and joined her. Even in death, 'old' was never a word I'd use to describe Ruby. Crazy? Yes. Wild? Definitely. Silly? For sure.

Ruby grinned and clasped her hands in her lap as she stared me down. "Now, let's talk about why I can go outside with you and where we're going."

I'd forgotten about that detail from my ventures out to the mysterious car parked behind my house. "Have you tried to leave again?"

"Oh, heck yes. I tried to leave last night to go down to Tip 'Em Back, but it was a no-go."

Pursing my lips together, I tried not to smile. My

guess was that a bar wouldn't be at the top of the list for most grandmas.

"Well, today we should go see Stan. Mr. Gonzalez fought with him before he checked in, and we agreed we need to find out who killed him."

"Sure. Sounds good. Where else are we going?"

I narrowed my gaze on her. "I... I don't know, Ruby. Did you have somewhere in mind, like the bar?"

"Well, I'm glad you asked, but I decided the bar would be pretty boring if I can't drink and talk to anyone, but it might be fun to go another time and just listen in on conversations. For today, I was thinking we could take the ATV out for a spin."

My heart sank and I realized I'd have to tell her I'd unloaded her beloved ATV a while back. The sale had been a spur of a moment thing. Shortly after Jack opened his business, I'd been at Darling's Diner and he'd come in to introduce himself. He'd mentioned he was looking to buy used ATVs. He'd handed me the cash and I'd taken him to the storage facility where it had been housed. "I... I had to sell it, Ruby. I needed the money."

"Dang it!" she yelled, her brow furrowed. "I was afraid you were going to say something like that! You haven't mentioned Flash at all."

Leave it to Ruby to name her ATV.

"We can rent one!" I blurted, wanting to please her. "We'll rent one from Jack!"

"Who's that?"

"Jumping Jack's Jeep Tours," I said, but her brow

still pinched in confusion, and I realized she didn't know him. He'd opened up his shop shortly after I arrived. Even though I talked him up to all my guests, I could see Ruby hadn't paid much attention. She had called it selective hearing while alive. "He rents ATVs and does jeep tours. We'll see him this afternoon after we talk to Stan."

"Okay," she agreed with a nod. "You should think about getting another ATV, though. You know how I love to ride them." She stood and stretched her arms to the sides. "Give me a holler when you're ready to hit the road."

As she faded away, I realized life outside of these four walls had changed, and I had no idea how Ruby would take it.

Why was she stuck on this plane? She had said she'd been told the reason but hadn't heard most of it.

Although I was really beginning to enjoy having her around, it wasn't fair to her. Once we'd solved the murder, I needed to find a way to get her to her final resting place.

For now, I'd make her happy and rent the dang ATV... after we visited As the Pins Drop.

CHAPTER 8

The bowling alley sat up the road about a mile, and with it being such a nice day, I decided to walk. Ruby strolled next to me humming a tune, something by *Lynyrd Skynyrd*, if my memory of our summers together served me correctly.

"What a beautiful day," she said, lifting her face to the sun. "I wish I could feel the heat on my skin. Being dead makes me pretty pale, and I always looked better with a tan."

I laughed, despite the fact I must have seemed insane to anyone paying me any attention.

"Where did that cute little restaurant go that used to be here?" She stopped in front of what was now a jewelry shop. "I loved their BLT sandwiches."

"I'm not sure when they closed," I said. "Maybe two years ago?"

"Oh, Bernie! Look at that mood ring!"

After stepping up to the window next to her, I

followed to where her ghostly hand pointed. The large, pale oval shined a greenish hue.

"You need to buy that," she said. "Dang it all, how I wish I was alive so I could wear it!"

The longing in her gaze brought tears to my eyes. Ruby loved to live, and it once again crushed me she had been caught in this strange middle area between life and death.

But, I certainly didn't need a mood ring. "I don't think—"

"Don't say no, Bernie! Do it for me! Let me live vicariously through you!"

Nothing like a little guilt to sway my decision. "Okay, fine," I replied with a huff. "Come on."

A woman who reminded me of a younger Ruby greeted us with a smile when we entered. Her long, blonde hair hung to her waist and she wore a flowy tie-dye dress.

"I'm interested in the big mood ring," I said, pointing to the window display.

"Look at all the pretties!" Ruby exclaimed. "Oh, my word! It's probably a good thing I'm dead or I'd have to find a rich boyfriend to afford everything I want!"

I pursed my lips as I tried on the ring. It fit perfectly and when I stretched out my hand in front of me, it looked like it belonged on my finger. "What do you think?" I asked.

"It looks great!" the woman behind the counter said, surprising me because I hadn't been talking to her.

"Oh, that's definitely a keeper," Ruby said. "It was made for you."

The oval remained blue and I smiled at the saleswoman. "What does the blue color mean?"

"Let me get you a chart," she said, turning away from us for a brief moment while she pulled open a drawer. "Here it is."

Ruby glanced over my shoulder as I read the paper. The ring remained in the blue range, meaning peace, happiness and relaxation. "See? I'm a good influence on you," Ruby said. "You're as calm as an ocean inlet on a clear day."

"Yes," I said. "Apparently so."

"I'm sorry? Apparently what?" the salesperson asked, her brow pinched in confusion.

"Apparently... this is a wonderful ring for me," I replied with a grin as the ring turned gold, which according to the chart, meant nervousness. *No one can hear Ruby but you. Don't talk to her in public.*

I paid for the ring and we were back out onto the sidewalk strolling toward the bowling alley. If there wasn't a murder hanging over our heads, it would have been easy to relax and enjoy the day with my ghost.

We stopped in front of As the Pins Drop, and I glanced at my ring, which had turned black. I pulled the chart from my pocket. Stress. How very accurate.

"Just go in and talk to him," Ruby encouraged. "What's he going to do? Beat you with a bowling ball?"

"I hadn't thought of that," I muttered. "But now that you bring it up, it's a possibility."

"You'll be fine. Besides, I'll be there for moral support."

That wouldn't do me much good, but I appreciated the thought.

Ruby went a few steps ahead of me and ghosted through the door. Seconds later, she was snapped back to my side.

"What was that all about?" I asked.

"It seems I can't go more than fifteen feet away from you outside the house," she replied. "I love you, but it's really quite annoying. I feel like you've got me on some leash I can't see."

"I'm sorry," I muttered as I opened the door, although, I wasn't really sure what to be sorry for. I'd done nothing to put Ruby into her predicament.

The bowling alley smelled like oil and feet. Right by the door stood a glass case showcasing bowling trophies, as well as military accolades. A few of the lanes were taken and balls whizzed down them, crashing into the pins. I'd never been one for bowling. In fact, I'd only participated one time, and it hadn't gone well. In my early twenties, I was on a date, and he thought it would be funny to place a little oil on the bottom of my shoes before giving them to me. After I put them on and stood up, I immediately went crashing to the floor and broke my arm. Once he admitted what he'd done, I never saw him again. At thirty-five, I'd seriously dated exactly four men, and found I was happiest when I was single. Ruby would tell me I just hadn't found the right guy, but I was beginning to wonder if such a thing existed for me... and if I even wanted to bother to look.

I walked over to the counter and realized I had no idea who Stan was. Since I didn't bowl and he had never needed a Bed and Breakfast, our paths hadn't crossed that I knew of.

"I'm looking for Stan," I said with a grin to the man in his forties behind the counter.

"Who wants to know?" he asked, his voice gruff and unfriendly.

"That's him," Ruby said. "His dad used to run this place. This boy was a jerk growing up and hasn't changed a lick. He's harmless, though. I used to buy my marijuana from him back in the good old days when I had a pulse."

"My name's Bernadette Maxwell," I said. "I own the bed and breakfast about a mile down the street. I was hoping I could talk to Stan for a moment."

He ran a hand over his already slicked back hair, and I swear he sucked in his stomach. "What do you need from me, Bernadette?" I noted his tone had changed. Was he flirting with me?

"Well, I understand you had a confrontation with one of my customers, and I wanted to find out your side of the story."

"Is your place really haunted?" he asked.

I glanced over at Ruby, who had perched herself on top of the counter. She rolled her eyes and shrugged, as if she didn't care how I answered.

"I believe it is," I said. "And most of my guests do as well. Strange things happen that can't be explained."

"That's what I've heard. I'd like to stay there some-time. Maybe we can trade. I'll give you a bowling session, and you let me stay the night."

"Can you tell me about your altercation with Mr. Gonzalez?" I asked, smiling. I'd never take that deal.

"Sure. The guy can't drive worth a darn. Cut me off on the highway, sent me into the ditch and dinged my bumper. I could have been killed. When I realized he was going to Sedona, I decided to give him a piece of my mind and get his insurance information."

"And that's when you followed him to my place?"

"Yeah," Stan replied, puffing out his chest. "Parked right behind him and told him he better learn to watch where he was going."

Stan's story didn't add up. Darla had said Mr. Gonzalez had a smoothie when he checked in.

"And he didn't go anywhere before arriving at my house?" I asked.

Stan shook his head, but then slammed his hand on the counter. "No, I was wrong. He went to Sarah's Smoothies. I didn't want to confront him there in front of everyone and embarrass him, just make him aware he was a horrible driver and get my bumper repaired. So I waited when it could just be the two of us."

"More like he didn't want to risk getting his butt kicked during the confrontation in front of the towns-people," Ruby said, floating down to stand next to me.

"He's just like his father. A lot of bark and no bite. Talks a tough game, but you could take him on."

I nodded but kept my focus on Stan. "So he went to Sarah's and then to my place."

"Yep."

"Got it. Thank you for your time."

As I turned to leave, Stan called, "How come I never see you around? You don't come in to bowl."

Glancing at the lanes, I shook my head. "Bowling isn't my thing."

"That's too bad. You should come in and try it. We've got a ladies' league. I can also give you private lessons, free of charge."

Eew.

"No, thanks," I said with a wave. "I'll have to pass on that."

"Why are you asking so many questions about that guy?" Stan yelled. "Did he do something?"

I turned around and walked back to the counter. "He died."

Stan's face flickered from surprise to curiosity. "How? When?"

"At some point yesterday, and the police aren't sure how. They're thinking he was poisoned."

The bluster he'd demonstrated earlier slowly leaked out of him. When he exhaled, I noted that he most certainly had been sucking in his gut. "Wow. Well... uh, that's too bad."

"You can read about it in the paper," I said.

"Okay. Thanks."

Once again, I headed for the door with my ghost in tow.

"What do you think about him?" Ruby asked. "Do you think he offed the guy?"

I waited until we were outside before answering. "I don't see how. Sheriff Walker said he thought Mr. Gonzalez died from poisoning. Unless Stan put something in his drink during the argument..."

"Like I said, all bark and no bite. Perhaps even a bit of a bully, just like his father. Now tell me, why don't you like bowling, Bernie?"

I quietly relayed my story, which sent Ruby into fits of laughter.

"Oh, Bernie," she said through her gasps, "I'm sorry to hear that, but dang it, I wish I could have seen it. Did you get back at him? Put saran wrap over his toilet? Sugar in his gas tank?"

"No, I never did anything about it."

Ruby shook her head. "Rule number one of life: You can't allow people to get away with garbage like that."

My mother had said the opposite—that I should let it go, which was the advice I had followed, but now regretted. I'd spent more than a few hours planning my retaliation for the oily shoes. "You're right," I said, sighing. "I should have gotten revenge at the time."

"Promise me you won't let something like that go again. I mean, it's a funny joke, but the fact you got hurt... there's no humor in that. He should have gotten his comeuppance."

As always, Ruby was correct.

"Where to now?" I asked as we headed down the sidewalk.

"You promised me an ATV ride."

"That's right. I did make that promise. So, I guess the next stop is Jumping Jack's."

"I can't wait!"

We took our time getting to Jack's, stopping to do a little more window shopping and enjoying the day. Yet, in the back of my mind, I wondered if Stan did have something to do with José Gonzalez's death. Had that been guilt I'd seen on Stan's face toward the end of the conversation, or sadness that the man had died? Was there really a difference? Maybe the fight had been worse than Darla had let on and Stan had somehow slipped something in Mr. Gonzalez's drink.

Or perhaps I was letting my imagination get the best of me.

I needed to find the murderer so the police wouldn't accuse me.

CHAPTER 9

"Oh, my goodness, Bernie," Ruby said breathlessly, walking a slow circle around Jack, her eyes as bright as the sun. "He's gorgeous. Why aren't you dating him again?"

My cheeks heated as I tried to ignore her while my heart thundered.

"He's got to be the best-looking man in Sedona," she continued. "Maybe even the state."

She was right. Jack's wavy brown hair, deep green eyes, and megawatt smile definitely could earn him the title.

He was also one of the biggest womanizers this town had ever seen. With no qualms about dating as many women as he wanted at one time, he'd started more than one fight between the ladies in town. Frankly, I tended to avoid anything resembling a date with him. I didn't want some other woman coming at me because I had taken her man, or some nonsense like that. Why get emotionally caught up with someone who had no regard for others? Jack was nice and I did like him, but that was where the relationship began and ended.

"Bernie? What's up?" Jack asked for the second time, his eyes squinting against the sun. "Are you okay?" I hadn't been able to answer the first because my grandmother's chatter had distracted me.

I noticed his jeans had a red tint to them, which most likely came from the red dirt in our area. He must have been lying on the ground working on one of his ATVs or jeeps.

"Yes. I'm sorry. I wanted to rent an ATV for a couple of hours."

Glancing around the parking lot, I noted there weren't any. Business had been good this afternoon for Jack. In reality, I didn't mind the idea of taking a seat and staring at him for a period of time, but that would be awkward.

"Well, I'm out of stock today, but I've got some free ones tomorrow. Will that work?"

Ruby's shoulders sagged, but she nodded. "The dead can't be picky. Besides, it'll give me something to look forward to."

"That'll work," I replied. "Some time in the afternoon would be best."

Mornings were for cleaning rooms, hopefully getting in a workout, and serving my customers' breakfast. More time opened up for me during the hour after lunch.

Jack's grin widened, and my knees weakened. Ruby was right. No one should be that good looking. "Let's go inside and get the paperwork filled out."

I followed him with Ruby at my side. "He sure fills out those jeans nicely. If only I were alive, I'd—"

"Stop it," I whispered, my cheeks flaming with embarrassment even though he couldn't hear her. "Please."

"Did you say something?" Jack asked over his shoulder.

I shook my head. "No. Just clearing my throat."

Jack's office included a desk and some pictures of the Sedona mountains along with the head of a deer, and I altered my stare. I hated hunting but understood some relied on it to feed their families. I just didn't understand the joy some found while killing.

The space couldn't be more than twenty-by-twenty. A hallway led to a space in back, but I'd never ventured down there.

"In all seriousness, Bernie, why don't you ask him out?" Ruby asked as I sat down in front of the desk.

Ignoring her, I smiled as Jack handed me a clipboard and pen. I scribbled down my information while making a mental note to tell her later I would never date him and he'd always remain in the friendship zone with me.

"Where you headed to tomorrow?" Jack asked. "It's not very often we get someone looking to ride by themselves. You burying a body or something up in the mountains?"

I laughed because my story was almost as absurd—my dead grandmother wanted a ride. "I haven't been in a number of years and I thought it would be fun."

"Make sure you're careful up there," Jack said. "Take your phone."

"I think he wants to go with you, Bernie," Ruby said as she stood behind him. "He seems concerned about you being out in the wild by yourself."

Ruby didn't know Jack dated a lot of women in this town, just not me. He'd never asked me out, and that was okay. My life was busy and full without having a man around.

"I have an idea," Jack said, folding his hands on top of the desk. "Why don't I go with you?"

"Yes!" Ruby shouted. "Bernie and Jack, sitting on an ATV, k-i-s-s-i-n-g. First comes love, then comes... "

Should I be flattered or horrified he wanted to join me? Maybe if I didn't have Ruby hanging around it wouldn't have been a big deal, but her constant chatter made it impossible to concentrate on anyone else.

But on the other hand, Jack and I had been friends for two years. We'd just never gone out. And riding ATVs together wouldn't exactly be considered a date.

"There are some new trails that are pretty fun, and I'd be happy to show them to you."

"If you don't say yes, I'm denouncing you as my granddaughter," Ruby said, resting her ghostly face on his shoulder.

Jack's nose crinkled and he glanced around. "That's weird. For a second, I thought I smelled marijuana."

Ruby jumped up onto the small desk between us and began to dance. "Say yes, say yes," she chanted. I tried not to stare at her, and realized the only way she'd stop her shenanigans was if I did agree to have Jack come with me.

"That sounds like fun," I said loudly, hoping she'd quiet down.

"The marijuana or the ride?" Jack asked with a chuckle.

I grinned at his cute dimples and wondered how many women in town had given them a quick squeeze. Jack was charming, and he knew it. "The ride."

Ruby floated off the desk and stood next to me, also smiling. It seemed she'd figured out the more obnoxious she became, the more it pressed me to do exactly what she wanted, and that didn't bode well for me.

Jack and I discussed the time, and then I stood to leave. "Thanks again. I'll see you tomorrow afternoon."

"Looking forward to it, Bernie!" he called as I closed the door.

"You have to stop being so loud," I muttered, once we were back on the street.

"Why? You're the only one who can hear me."

"Because you make it so I can't think straight."

"I'm so excited he's coming with us tomorrow!"

"Listen to me," I said, glancing around before coming to a halt. "I am not dating Jack, nor will I ever. The guy is the local heartbreaking Romeo and I don't want any part of it. Do you understand?"

Ruby's face fell. "Is he really?"

"Yes."

"I should have seen that, Bernie. Those dimples were a dead giveaway. Rule number two-hundred-seventy-eight of life: don't date womanizers with dimples."

With a sigh, I continued on my way, Ruby at my side. She was so interested in finding me a date and riding ATVs, it was like she'd completely forgotten a body had been found in my house and that I'd lied to the police. I had to stay on task and find the murderer.

Sarah's Sensational Smoothies sat just down the street from Jack's. As usual, the line was out the door. As we waited, I debated whether to get a lemongrass and blueberry one for myself. The stress of Mr. Gonzalez's demise ate at my stomach, so a shot of probiotics would probably be an excellent idea.

Thankfully, Sarah and her two employees were fast and efficient and the line moved quickly. She smiled when we arrived at the counter. In her fifties, she had curly blonde hair she wore in a cute bob and big blue eyes. Her tanned face indicated she spent a lot of time outdoors when not working.

"What can I get for you, Bernie?" she asked. "The usual?"

"Get the peanut butter and chocolate with extra whipped cream," Ruby said. "That sounds amazing."

"Yes. My usual please," I said.

"Lemongrass and blueberry coming right up!" Sarah said. "Do you want a shot of probiotics as well?"

"Please. Thank you."

"Oh, my word," Ruby whispered. "I thought you were allowing me to live vicariously through you. I'd never drink that garbage."

"It's good," I murmured. "And buying a ring is one thing, but taking care of my nutritional needs is something quite different. This is a wholesome choice for me while *your* preference is garbage."

"My choice is living in the moment and enjoying every second to the fullest, Bernie. That's rule number two. You *will* die, so you might as well appreciate life a little bit each day."

While chewing on my lip, I considered her words. The chocolate and peanut butter did sound delicious, but the blueberry and lemongrass one was so much better for me. Did I really enjoy it though? Not as much as I would the other, that's for certain. Perhaps next time I'd venture into the sugar-filled, fat-laden treat.

"I heard about that guy they found at your place," Sarah said, lowering her voice to almost a whisper. "I'm sorry to hear about it. I hope it doesn't affect your business. What happened to him?"

"They think he was poisoned. Listen, did you know he came here before he checked in at my place?"

Her eyes widened and she shook her head. "No! I had no idea!"

"Yes. Apparently, he checked in carrying one of your smoothies. Did anything strike you as weird about him? Do you even remember him? Middle-aged guy with black hair, a little overweight?"

"Oh, my gosh. We were so busy yesterday. I wouldn't remember if I waited on my own mother."

Frustration welled within me and I sighed. How was I going to find out anything about Mr. Gonzalez if she didn't even remember him? "Have the cops been here? Have they told you anything?"

"No. Do you think they're going to assume I had something to do with it?"

"Why would you think that?"

Even though the customer voices were loud all around us, it was like the two of us had been sucked into a strange time warp and silence surrounded us as we stared at each other.

She shrugged and seemed to be struggling to find the right words. "I just... I just thought..."

"It's okay," I said, gently laying my hand on hers. "Don't worry about things until you have something to worry about."

"I just told you that yesterday, didn't I?" Ruby asked.

"If people think I had something to do with his death, it could be the end of my business," Sharon continued as tears welled in her eyes. "I'm sorry the man died, but I didn't have anything to do with it."

"Of course not," I said, surprised by her emotion. Frankly, it made her seem somewhat guilty, or maybe she truly was worried about her business. I hadn't considered the consequences of a dead man being found in my bed and breakfast, so I began to worry as well. What if my business took a dive? I may not have a business if the police thought I had anything to do with Mr. Gonzalez's death.

Sarah's eyes widened and she gasped while looking over my shoulder. I turned to find Adam and the sheriff strolling in.

"Call me when they leave," I said to Sarah. "Let me know what they say."

She nodded and resembled someone about to be led to the guillotine. What was she so freaked out about if she didn't have anything to do with the death?

I smiled as the police approached the counter.

"Ladies," Sheriff Walker said, tipping his cowboy hat. "I'd like to speak to you privately, Sarah, if you don't mind."

"Of course," she whispered, taking off her apron and coming around the counter.

The three disappeared down a back hallway to what I assumed was Sarah's office, but not before Adam glanced over at me with... pity? Had I read that right?

Thankfully, Sarah had her two employees to help her out with the continuous crowd behind me. I weaved my way through the people and back out onto the sidewalk, Ruby in tow.

"What's her deal?" Ruby asked. "She's acting guilty."

"I agree."

"Do you think she poisoned him?"

"I don't know, Ruby."

"You need to look at that police report. See if they know for sure that's how he kicked the bucket."

"I agree, but did you see that stare Adam just gave me?"

"No, but I bet he's looking for some action."

"It wasn't that," I said, rolling my eyes. "It's like he felt sorry for me or something."

"You got it all! Brains, a stable income, looks, a pert butt... why in the world would he feel sorry for you?"

A good question, but I didn't have an answer and I doubted I'd ever find one. "I have no idea. For now, let's head home."

CHAPTER 10

*W*ell, I certainly didn't have to wait long for my answer. I had it the second I rounded the corner to my street. The stare had definitely been pity.

Three cop cars lined up in front of my house and the front door hung open wide.

"Oh, no," I whispered as I broke into a run. Ruby trailed behind me sort of floating while trying to catch her footing, as though I was pulling her on the invisible leash she'd mentioned.

"Would you slow down?"

But I couldn't. First and foremost, my door was open, which meant Elvira could escape at any time. If my cat went missing, the police were going to have a lot more to worry about than the dead guy found upstairs.

"What's going on here?" I asked as I jogged up the

walk to the policeman waiting by the front door. "This is my house. What are you doing?"

"We have a warrant, Ms. Maxwell."

"A warrant for what?"

"To search your house. It's now the scene of a murder investigation."

I stared at his pudgy face with mirrored sunglasses and couldn't read him in any way—a guy just doing his job. "Where's my cat? Please tell me you didn't let her out."

"Haven't seen one leave the premises."

How terribly unhelpful.

"Can I go in? Please? I need to find Elvira and make sure she doesn't get out."

Sedona sat up in the mountains and we had all sorts of wildlife hanging around that would appreciate Elvira as their meal: coyotes, bobcats and hawks, just to name a few.

"You can enter and sit on the couch with the others," he said, stepping to the side.

"The others? Who are they?"

"That would be your guests," Ruby said, standing in the doorway. "They're sitting on the couch. The fuzz is searching every room, bagging stuff up. It's a mess."

"The Thompsons?" the cop asked incredulously. "Surely you remember they rented a room from you?" Of course. In all the happenings of the day, I'd forgotten about them. "You can go sit with them."

I nodded and entered, glancing everywhere for

Elvira. I turned to the cop. "Can I please ask if anyone's seen my cat?"

After unclipping a radio from his belt, he spoke into it. "Anyone seen a cat around?"

"Negative."

"Yup. In the downstairs bedroom under the bed. Dang thing about clawed out my eyeball during my search."

"There you go," the cop said.

"Thank you." At least Elvira was okay and I secretly liked she'd taken a swipe at the cop. "Can I go grab her?"

"Negative. Sit on the couch, Ms. Maxwell."

"Then don't let her out of the house." He pulled down his glasses and glared at me, thoroughly exasperated. "Please? I can't lose my cat."

He nodded and pointed toward the living room.

Somewhere along the way, Ruby had disappeared. As I walked into the living room, the Thompsons stared at me accusingly. I had told them nothing happened in the bedroom, and now my house was being tossed by the cops. They didn't have to be overly smart to figure out I'd lied to them.

"This is an interesting turn of events," Bobbie said as I sat down. "What the heck is going on? A murder? Here? Is that correct? That's what the police told us."

I nodded and glanced down at my clasped hands. My new ring had turned black, the sign of stress. Why wasn't I surprised?

"You owe us an explanation," Bob said. "They're

going through our things and we've been caught up in something awful. I don't know if we would have stayed with you if we'd known there'd been a *murder* in the house!"

I cleared my throat and considered my words carefully. "Yes, a man died in that room upstairs. At the time, the police thought he'd been poisoned, but they didn't mention a murder."

"Is there a difference?" Bobbie asked. "I mean, he was poisoned! That equates to murder in my book."

"People also commit suicide by drinking poison," I said. "So, I wasn't comfortable telling anyone what had happened until I knew the cause of death."

"Well, the police think that you had something to do with it, or they wouldn't be tearing apart your house," Bobbie growled. "This is unbelievable."

Guilt washed over me as I stared at my guests. Yes, they'd been in the wrong place at the wrong time, and now had become a part of this investigation. "I'm sorry you've been caught up in this. Honestly, I had no idea what was going on. I just knew a man died. I didn't know it was murder."

"It doesn't make any sense," Bobbie hissed. "Why in the world would someone check into a bed and breakfast to kill themselves? How silly."

"Actually, it's nothing new," Bob said, patting his wife's hand. "Oftentimes, people don't want their loved ones to find them, so they do check into hotels and such."

I narrowed my gaze on them as it occurred to me

they were supposed to be hiking and practicing yoga at Cathedral Rock. What had they done? Gone out there, stayed five minutes, and returned? The hike itself was a good couple of hours. "How was yoga at the vortex?"

"It was fine," Bob muttered.

But I also noted he wore jeans. I tried to recall him this morning, and I realized he had the same pants on then. Who did yoga in jeans? No one, that's who.

Something wasn't adding up with the two, and my guilt over the situation dissipated rather quickly.

"Mr. and Mrs. Thompson?" a cop called as he rounded the corner from the kitchen. "Could you please come in here?"

They rose from the couch and followed the police. I ground my jaw, wishing I could hear what they spoke about. Then, I realized I had my ghost.

"Ruby!" I whispered, springing to my feet. "Ruby! Come here! I need you!" I glanced around the room, waiting for her to make an appearance. Nothing. "Dang it, Ruby! Come here! Please!"

"Just yesterday you were telling me to go away," Ruby said as she pranced into the room, Elvira trailing behind her. "And now, here you are *begging* me to make an appearance. I feel like a movie star or something!"

"Go into the kitchen and find out what that cop is asking the Thompsons!" I whispered as I picked up Elvira.

"Not even a thank you for wrangling your cat?"

"Thank you!" I hissed, trying not to roll my eyes. "Please, go find out what's being said!"

Ruby turned, tossed her ponytail over her shoulder, and left for the kitchen.

"I'm sorry about all the people in your house," I whispered to Elvira as I curled up on the couch with her. She began to purr but kept her gaze firmly on the hallway leading to the kitchen, her ears twitching with every sound wafting down from upstairs.

My phone rang, and I quickly answered it.

"We see you have company," the mechanical voice said. I gasped as fear gripped my chest. "Keep them away from the car."

"How do I do that?" I whispered.

"We suggest you send them looking somewhere else besides your home."

Tears welled in my eyes as I glanced around my living room. Every drawer had been opened, my things strewn about. They'd even poked around in the fireplace—the logs I'd arranged so artfully now lay scattered.

"Just come get your stupid car," I hissed.

"We will in time. Deflect the police."

The line went dead as a cop walked into the living room carrying a box filled with all my cleaning supplies without even glancing at me. How the heck was I supposed to tidy up the rooms now? I'd have to hurry to the store for more supplies.

Whoever was responsible for Mr. Gonzalez's death watched the house closely and rankled my nerves. How was I supposed to keep the cops away from the car? They acted like I was some career criminal with a lot of experience with the police and investigations. Boy, were they wrong. Straight and narrow was my path. I kept my head down and my nose clean. What the heck had I gotten myself into?

Ruby appeared a few minutes later. Too bad she wasn't alive. The mess seemed to be perfect for her lane in life.

"What are they saying?" I whispered as she sat down next to me.

"That they're on their honeymoon and they're absolutely mortified by the utter chaos—their words, not mine— they've found themselves in. They plan on leaving as soon as the police let them." She used her hand to fan her face, then brought it to her forehead and sighed, very silent-movie-like. "The drama in there is thicker than melted chocolate."

I ignored her theatrics. "Honeymoon? They didn't mention anything about it when they checked in."

"That's what they told the cops."

On my reservation form, I specifically ask if guests are celebrating anything special during their stay with me. They had checked the "no" box. Perhaps they didn't want to have a big deal made out of their trip? Or were they lying to the police? But what would be the motive?

And what had happened to their day trip of yoga and hiking? They could have only been gone an hour or two, tops.

When they emerged from the kitchen with the cop behind them, each shot me a glare. The officer motioned me to follow him as the Thompsons went outside with Bobbie wiping her teary eyes. *Not buying your drama, lady.*

I stood and took Elvira with me for emotional support, feeling as if I were being led to a firing squad for a crime I hadn't committed.

"Sit down, please," he said gruffly, motioning to my kitchen table.

Once we were situated, I studied his brown and gray hair that desperately needed a cut, and his hard, no-nonsense gaze. Placing him somewhere in his forties or fifties, I realized he'd run out of patience long ago.

"So, tell me why you lied to the police yesterday."

He didn't waste time reminding me of my offense or bother to introduce himself. However, me telling the truth that I had my dead grandmother's ghost floating around talking to me wouldn't bode well for me either. "I didn't lie... Officer Mitchell." Thank goodness for nametags. "I lost track of time and made a mistake."

"Uh huh. Here's what I think happened. I think you killed that man."

My hand moved over Elvira in a soothing rhythm that I hoped hid my trembling fingers. "I didn't kill anyone," I said, my voice soft despite my panic and desire to scream anxiously. "I wasn't even here when he checked in."

He narrowed his gaze on me. "Where were you?"

And here it was. My chance to throw out a bunch of names that deflected from them focusing on me.

"I flew in from Louisiana and grabbed the shuttle

from Phoenix. I told the sheriff this yesterday. I still have the receipts if you'd like to see them."

"Where are they?"

"On my bedroom dresser."

He unhooked the radio from his belt. "Troy, do you see receipts on the dresser for a flight and shuttle yesterday?"

It was bad enough the police were tearing apart my house, but queasiness set in at the thought of a man I didn't know rummaging through my private sanctuary and touching my personal things.

"Yup. Already bagged them."

After setting down the radio, he took a couple of notes and then glared at me again. "Where's your boarding pass for the flight?"

"I erased it from my phone on the drive up from Phoenix," I said. I may have the receipts that I paid for the airline and the shuttle, but I never in a million years imagined I'd need to keep the boarding pass. I liked my phone the way I liked my house and my life in general: neat and tidy. I always erased things I didn't need.

"If you weren't here, who checked him in? Do you have an employee?"

"My friend Darla was here in the morning."

"Darla who?"

"Darla Darling."

"The woman who owns the diner?"

"Yes."

He scratched her name down and I realized I'd just thrown her under the proverbial bus... unless, of course, she'd killed Mr. Gonzalez. Then, that meant I'd just handed the murderer over to the police. Either way I didn't think Darla would be pleased with me but hopefully she'd understand that I couldn't lie to the police. Again.

"He also had a fight with Stan from As the Pins Drop," I continued, desperate to take the focus off me. Besides, I didn't feel bad about putting Stan in their crosshairs. Call me cruel, but I hadn't particularly liked the guy.

"How do you know?"

"Darla saw them argue and I talked to Stan about it. He said Mr. Gonzalez was a bad driver and they had words over a near-crash on the highway."

"Why didn't you tell us any of this yesterday?"

"I didn't know any of it then."

He tapped his pen against the pad of paper. "I feel as though you are sending me on a wild goose chase to take the focus off yourself."

I wasn't sure what to say to that. Shrugging, I wished I could think of another name to toss his way. They were already questioning Sarah, so it seemed overkill to mention her again. "I wasn't in town in the morning hours. I didn't have anything to do with his death."

"What about that afternoon? While you were sleeping? Did you lock the front door?"

I'd given that a great deal of thought, and the answer was probably no, but I couldn't be sure. I had been quite distracted by discovering my ghost. "I'm not positive, but I don't think so."

That also added another layer of diversion off me. Someone could have waltzed right in and killed the man. But why only him? Why not me as well? And if that had been the case, why hadn't Ruby noticed? Perhaps she'd gone to her tunnel. I'd have to ask.

Sweat formed on my brow and I tried to wipe it away as nonchalantly as possible. My stress level climbed in minuscule amounts by the second.

"Anything else you'd like to share, Ms. Maxwell?"

His stare indicated he still thought I was guilty, but I smiled and shook my head, hoping I didn't break out into tears.

"We'll be out of your house soon. Until then, stay put either here or in the living room."

After he rose from the chair, I looked around my kitchen. Again, the drawers had been opened and everything emptied. If every room resembled what I'd already seen, it would take me hours, if not days, to put my home back together.

And it had become more apparent than ever that I needed to solve the case for two reasons: first, to avoid prison, and second, to keep breathing. I didn't want to become the next victim.

CHAPTER 11

"*R*uby, where were you yesterday afternoon when I lay down to take a nap?" I asked, picking up a dining room placemat from the floor and stacking it on top of the others. After counting once again, I realized I was still missing one from the set. Where had it gone?

"I went to my tunnel," she said. "After you finally noticed me and convinced yourself you'd gone bonkers, I became a little depressed." She sprawled out on the couch with Elvira lying at her feet. "I mean, I was your favorite grandma, and you weren't the least bit excited to see me."

"It's not every day I come across someone who's been dead for three years," I muttered as I glanced around for my missing placemat. Honestly, I became more irritated with those cops by the second. "I can't believe this mess."

"Why do you ask where I was?"

"What if someone marched in here and killed him? I was wondering why you didn't see them."

Footsteps sounded down the stairs and I turned to find the Thompsons. Both had their suitcases, and frankly, I was happy to see them leaving, even if it was one day early. I wouldn't want to be caught up in my life if I were them, and I'd also developed some serious trust issues because of their blatant lies to the police. The more distance they put between my house and their car, the happier I'd be.

"Oh, look. Liar One and Liar Two," Ruby said. "There's something rotten in the state of Denmark."

I glanced over at her, surprised by her Hamlet quote. Usually, she parroted Lynyrd Skynyrd or the Grateful Dead.

"W-we've decided we don't feel safe here," Bobbie said, smiling nervously. "We're going to leave town."

"I understand," I said. "I wish you safe travels."

The three of us stared at each other a minute, and I wasn't sure what they expected from me. A refund? A hug?

"We like you, Bernie," Bob said. "I'm not sure what you've gotten yourself into, but we hope you're careful."

"Yes," Bobbie agreed. "It would be a shame to see anything happen to you."

Chills ran over my skin and down my spine as they turned and headed for the front door. Had they wished me well, or had their words been a veiled threat?

"Oh, man, am I glad they're gone," Ruby said. "I hate liars."

"Me, too," I whispered. I particularly hated liars who threatened me, and I ran my palms over my arms to calm the chill. Then I hurried over and locked the front door.

"So, what's your plan now?" Ruby asked.

"The people called again about the car," I said.

"Why didn't you tell me about that?!" Ruby yelled, sitting upright. "What did they say?"

"The cops were here, and I thought it would seem weird to them if I started talking to my resident ghost."

"Okay, fine, I get it," Ruby said with a huff. "What did they want?"

"To remind me to stay away from the car, to make sure the cops didn't discover it and to give them a bunch of red herrings for the investigation."

"They're watching the house," Ruby murmured. "Very carefully. I wonder from where?"

"Unless it's one of the houses down the street, it has to be from the mountains. They can see the car out back. It's the only thing that makes sense."

"Agreed, Bernie. I wish we knew what was in that car."

"I do, too." Actually, I'd concocted a little plan to find out, but the execution was still fuzzy to me. Until I had it worked out, I didn't want to let Ruby in on my idea.

"What's your next step?" she asked.

"I don't know," I said with a shrug. "This place is a

mess, the police accused me of murder, and my life was threatened. I feel like I have to solve the case."

"And how do you plan on doing that?"

After picking up my phone, I glanced at my reservation app. No one would show for five days, but that didn't mean I couldn't have walk-ins. Cleaning up seemed important, especially if I was to have customers. But I could always hang out my *closed* shingle, leave the mess, and get on with trying to solve the crime.

"You need to figure out what the police know," Ruby said. "Go flirt with that young cop. What was his name?"

My cheeks heated and I glanced down at my ring. Red. I certainly didn't like my emotions being out in the open for everyone to see, so I pulled it off and shoved it in my pocket. "Adam."

"Go flirt with him," Ruby said as she stood and began twirling around. "Find out everything the cops know. Maybe it will help."

"I wish I wasn't a suspect," I muttered. "I mean, I wasn't even in town. I've told them that twice."

"You're a suspect because you lied to them," Ruby said as she sat down again next to Elvira. "And just because you have those receipts doesn't mean you've used them."

And here I thought they cleared me. I glanced over at my ghost, thoroughly confused. "Why would I buy a plane and shuttle ticket and not use them?"

"To give yourself an alibi."

I had the distinct feeling Ruby was speaking from experience. Did I want to know the story? Probably not.

"See, there was this married man I used to date," she began. "Now this was years ago. I was in my twenties and didn't know any better. I was young, selfish and very foolish. Rule number two of life: don't sleep with married men. It's wrong.

Anyway, he didn't want to leave his wife, which was fine with me. I didn't want a man around permanently, anyway. He used to tell his wife he was going away on business trips and he'd buy a plane ticket. Well, he'd come over to my house and we'd—"

"I get it," I said, holding up my hand. "I understand now. He had his alibi if his wife ever questioned him."

"Exactly," Ruby said, nodding. "And for the record, I only slept with two married men when I was alive. Way too much drama for me."

"Of course," I muttered with a sigh as I folded the napkins and set them back into the drawer. Ruby never suffered from guilt, unlike me. Sometimes I was riddled with it, even when I shouldn't be. "That's an expensive alibi."

"He had money to burn," Ruby said with a shrug. "And I was worth it."

I had thought the tickets cleared me, but she'd proven otherwise. No wonder the cops kept pestering me. They'd probably seen a guilty party pull out a plane ticket a half-dozen times to prove their innocence.

A half-hour later, I had the dining room put back

together and had started on the living room. My phone blared in the quiet, sending Elvira racing for the stairs, and I actually screamed I'd been so caught up in my own thoughts.

I picked up the device fully expecting a call from Sarah as she'd promised. I took a few deep breaths and tried to calm my thundering heart. The number was familiar.

"Hi, Darla," I said breathlessly.

"How dare you?" she hissed. "I cannot believe you!"

Uh-oh. "How dare I what?" Glancing around, I noted Ruby had once again disappeared.

"The police just left the diner, Bernie. They told me that you gave them my name and now I'm a suspect in your murder!"

Oh. Okay. I understood. "I didn't have a choice," I said. "They asked me who checked Gonzalez in, and I had to give them your name."

"You most certainly did *not* have to do that!" she yelled. "I had nothing to do with that man dying!"

"Darla, when I explained to them that I was in Louisiana, they asked who was taking care of my business for me. That was you. I couldn't lie."

"They came into my diner and stomped around like they owned the place!" she yelled, obviously not hearing my explanation. "Then they pulled me away from dinner preparation to talk to me, even though I explained I was busy and had nothing to do with the death!"

"I'm sorry, Darla. They were here at the house and—"

"And that's exactly where they should have stayed! I had customers clearing out! I lost money because of you!"

"Darla—"

"I did you a favor, and this is how you repay me? By throwing me under the bus? You aren't a friend, Bernadette Maxwell. In fact, don't ever call me again. You're dead to me."

She hung up and I stared at the phone, unable to believe the conversation. So what if the police upended her life for a few minutes? They were looking for a murderer, which was a little more important than her cutting lettuce for BLT sandwiches.

Unless she was guilty. Then she'd be terribly upset about the police poking around.

But how would she have murdered him?

She'd seen Mr. Gonzalez fighting with Stan out on the street. He'd come into the house and she'd checked him in. Perhaps she'd slipped something into his smoothie from Sarah's when he wasn't looking? But why? Had she known him? Had he been rude to her or done something inappropriate?

With a sigh, I sat down at the dining room table, ran my hand over the pristine, shiny wood, then rubbed my temples.

You're dead to me. Dang, that was harsh, and my chest began to ache as tears stung my eyes. How could my best friend say that to me? Perhaps Darla would calm down and realize I had no choice. I found her reaction over-exaggerated at best. As the tears spilled, I didn't know if they were from sadness, anger, or from feeling overwhelmed by my situation. Maybe a little of everything. Ruby appeared on the other side of the table after I slammed my hand down on the surface.

"What's got your knickers on fire?" she asked.

"I just got off the phone with Darla," I said, sniffing as I wiped my eyes. "She said I'm dead to her because I told the cops she checked Gonzalez in and they're now investigating her."

Ruby arched an eyebrow. "Wow. That's a little uncalled for and very rude. Why was she so upset?"

I shrugged and wiped my cheeks again. Stupid tears. I hated crying.

"Sounds like she's guilty or something," Ruby said.

"That's exactly what I thought. I don't understand how she would have poisoned him, or why."

"See? You need to go find out what the police know."

"It's not like I can waltz into the station and make demands for them to tell me everything."

"Of course you can't. Like I said, you need to be a little stealthier than that. You need to use your womanly wiles to get what you want."

I rolled my eyes. "That tactic went out of style years ago."

"Well, it should make a comeback. A bat of the eyelashes and a smile go a long way with men."

I stared at the table, unsure how to respond.

"But then again, so does a cheeseburger, beer, and a football game. You have to use what's at your disposal. Right now, you've got your looks. Go put them to work."

CHAPTER 12

$\mathcal{I}$ stood in front of the mirror and applied a little mascara, getting ready to go meet Adam.

"Definitely use more," Ruby said from the doorway behind me. "You want those baby blues to really pop."

With a sigh, I eyed myself critically. I also didn't want my eyelashes to resemble spider legs. "I think that's enough."

"Suit yourself. Add a little blush, though. You're looking a little tired and pale."

Understatement of the year. No matter how many deep breathing exercises I did, my mind kept racing and panic gripped my chest at my situation. Sleep did not come easily, and only in short fits.

I added the blush and returned to my bedroom. Standing in front of my closet, I decided to wear my *Pretty in Pink* T-shirt.

Ruby sighed and shook her head as I pulled it on.

"Seriously, Bernie? I know you have a thing for eighties movies, but that shirt has the sex appeal of a dead skunk. Find something with a little more cleavage."

"I don't have anything with cleavage," I muttered, becoming irritated with her. "This shirt will be fine."

"What if he doesn't like eighties movies? What if he's more of a nineties guy and prefers *Wayne's World* and *Dumb and Dumber* over Molly Ringwald?"

"Well, *Wayne's World* wasn't bad, so we can agree on that."

"Both movies deserve to go down in the history books as classics," she said with a chuckle. "Especially *Wayne's World*. Goodness, that was funny. But seriously, change your top."

I studied my reflection in the mirror and decided *Pretty in Pink* it was. "I'm wearing the dang shirt, Ruby. I don't want to look like I'm trying to impress him."

"Why not? Men like that stuff. Dress to impress and all that."

I sighed, finding it hard to believe a headache had already begun to form behind my eyes and I hadn't even left my bedroom yet. "Ruby..."

"Fine. Wear what you want."

"The only one I need to impress is myself."

"I agree, one hundred percent. However, flashing a little cleavage every now and then never hurt anyone."

She disappeared before I could argue.

With a sigh, I fed Elvira and grabbed a garlic and onion bagel for myself, missing the eggs and bacon Darla usually brought over whether I had guests or not.

I still didn't understand why she'd been so upset over a visit from the police, and that had been the main reason I'd remained awake most of the night. Could she have really been that rattled, or was she guilty of something?

Like me, Darla tended to suffer from a bit of anxiety every now and then, so maybe it had gotten the best of her. Hopefully, she'd call today and apologize for her outburst. Or perhaps I should give her a ring? Nope. I couldn't handle being yelled at again. No more tears for me.

And Sarah had never called after her confrontation with the police. Was she upset with me as well, or had she simply forgotten? It seemed like I was losing friends faster than greased lightning.

I quickly gave my teeth another brushing, not wanting to smell like garlic and onion when I spoke to Adam. My plan had been to slip out the front door and leave Ruby here since she was tethered to me outside the house. I didn't want her chattering over my shoulder while I met with Adam. After listening intently, I didn't hear her singing or talking to Elvira, so I figured she'd gone to her tunnel. I quietly hurried through the house, but when I rounded the corner, her ghostly form was standing by the front door with her arms crossed over her chest.

"You were going to leave me!" she shrieked. "I knew it!"

"N-no, I wasn't," I stammered, my face flushing from being caught in the lie.

"Yes, you were! I can tell by your cheeks!"

"Fine," I said with a sigh. "When we meet Adam, can you please not talk?"

"Why not?"

"Because you are *so* distracting!"

Her face fell as if I'd hurt her feelings. "I'm only trying to help you."

Now I felt even guiltier. "Look, I appreciate you wanting to help me, I really do. But when you start talking at the same time I'm trying to hold another conversation, it's difficult for me to split my concentration between you and the person I'm supposed to be talking to. I'm just not that talented."

Ruby nodded. "I understand. And I'll remain quiet."

"Okay. Thank you. Should we go?"

"Yes. Get me out of here. Please."

Relief swept through me as we exited the house. I needed Ruby for moral support and a future plan I was still trying to piece together, and I didn't want her upset with me as well. Darla's wrath still hurt.

"Another lovely day!" Ruby said, smiling, as we walked. "Although, I do wish we'd take your SUV instead. We could get there a lot faster."

"I need the exercise," I replied. "I haven't had much time to do anything."

"Murder investigations will do that to you. It'll be nice when we put all this behind us."

I couldn't agree more.

"Maybe we can have that dance party?" Ruby ventured.

With a smile, I nodded, although even thinking about having fun seemed like the wrong thing to do, especially if I could end up in prison for a crime I didn't commit.

Butterflies tickled my belly as we approached the police station. As a woman in her thirties—actually, closer to the forties—I shouldn't have been nervous at the thought of talking to a man, but here I was.

Before we entered, I whispered, "Remember, you need to be quiet, okay?"

"Quiet as the dead. That's me."

We stared at each other for a beat and then both burst out laughing. A few people glared at me like I was the local crazy person, but I couldn't stop.

"Oh, heck, that was funny," Ruby said. "Nothing like a good belly laugh. Best medicine in the world."

I wiped my eyes and hoped my mascara hadn't run down my face, but I did feel much better. Ruby was right about laughter being the best medicine.

"Go in there and slay that man with sexiness!" Ruby yelled as I pulled open the door.

I'd called early in the morning to find out Adam's work schedule, and learned his arrival should coincide with mine. That way, I wouldn't have to track him down if he was out on patrol.

"Is Adam in?" I asked the receptionist, a smiling woman in her sixties.

"One moment, dear." She stood slowly and disappeared around the corner, then came back a moment later. "He's on his way," she said with a wink.

I took a seat and waited patiently. The side door swung open and he strode out, each step exuding confidence. He didn't bother to try and hide his surprise when our gazes locked.

"Bernadette? What are you doing here?" He ran a hand through his blond hair and stared at me expectantly.

"I... I... um... was wondering if we could grab a cup of coffee or something."

His brow creased in confusion. "What for?"

"I wanted to talk to you about Mr. Gonzalez." I batted my eyelashes, hoping I was doing it right.

"Do you have something in your eye?" Adam asked. "Should I get you a tissue or something?"

Yes, that's me. Sexy to the bone.

"No, I'm fine," I said, my cheeks heating. "What about that coffee? I'm buying."

"If we're going to talk about the case, we should do it in an interrogation room. It should be a formal discussion."

Pursing my lips together, I had no idea how to answer, and I glanced over at Ruby hoping she'd help me out of this one. Instead, she stared at me like she would a strange animal in the zoo, as if she couldn't quite comprehend my awkwardness.

"Should we head back?" Adam asked.

"Don't let him take you back there, Bernie. It's one door closer to jail. Tell him police stations and Sheriff Walker scare you," Ruby finally blurted. "Tell him it's not official. You just want to talk about it and you

THE GUEST IS A GONER

aren't expecting him to give up anything about the investigation, even though that's exactly what you're asking him to do."

I repeated Ruby's words and Adam's features softened.

"Well, I certainly don't want to put you in an uncomfortable position," he said. "I guess a coffee wouldn't hurt. I like your shirt, by the way. Great movie."

"Thanks!" I said, sticking out my tongue out at Ruby when he turned his back to me.

Relief swept through me as we exited the building with my ghost trailing behind us, humming a tune I didn't recognize.

Canyon Coffee was just a few doors down and Adam held the door open for me. I inhaled deeply as the smells of coffee, sugar, and cinnamon engulfed us. Overstuffed leather couches and magazine racks littered the room, the walls had been painted in warm colors, and a large fireplace sat in the middle of the room. The place reminded me of a cozy living room; it was one of my favorite stores, especially in the winter months.

We waited in line and once we got up to the counter, Ruby said, "I know I'm not supposed to say anything to you, but if you don't get one of those strawberry custard doodads, you are foolish."

I glanced over at the display case and my mouth began to water. Usually, I avoided looking in there as I didn't want to tempt myself. Yet, one of those strawberry custard doodads did look delicious. The calories alone would mean I probably couldn't eat the rest of the day.

"Live a little bit," Ruby said. "I can see you want it. One isn't going to kill you or put you up a pant size."

Before I knew it, I had ordered the treat and a coffee, then practically salivated all over it as we walked over to a couch and sat down. The first bite caused me to groan and quickly take a second.

Adam burst out laughing. "I wish I'd gotten one of those now."

"It's delicious," I said, covering my mouth with my fingers. "I haven't had any sugar in months."

"Uh-oh. Between the caffeine and the sugar, are we going to have to scrape you off the ceiling?"

"Let's hope not," I replied, then took a sip of coffee.

We sat in silence for a few moments as I scarfed down my strawberry delectable that I swore was made by angels and dropped down from the heavens. I wasn't sure how to bring up the murder, but thankfully, Adam did.

"So, what do you want to know?" he asked. "I'll tell you what I can."

I'd actually given his question a lot of thought and it frightened me that someone could have been in my house without me knowing it. "I know the sheriff said he thought Mr. Gonzalez was poisoned. I was wondering how that happened."

Adam furrowed his brow. "Well, he ingested something."

"So there weren't any needle marks or anything like that?"

It didn't seem a struggle had taken place in the bedroom where he'd died. Nothing had been out of place, but I needed to be sure.

"No. We think the poison was slipped into the smoothie cup. Why do you want to know?"

"I was scared that someone had come into my house while I slept and poisoned him. I imagine if that were the case, the room would have been trashed from a fight, because who's going to sit around and allow someone to stick a needle in them?"

"Ah, I see," Adam said. "Well, we don't know who put the poison into his cup. There are few times it could have happened after he arrived in town."

From what I knew, it could have been during his visit to the smoothie shop, his altercation with Stan, or when he'd checked in with Darla. Of course, the sheriff's office had made it clear they suspected me as well since I'd been alone in the house with him and had lied, thanks to Ruby.

Speaking of which...

I glanced around the immediate area to find her hovering over an older woman's shoulder on the next couch reading the paper. "Lady, you read slower than a blind slug," she muttered as she waited for the woman to flip the page.

Turning back to Adam, I met his gaze. "Am I still a suspect?"

Jeez, he had prettiest, blue eyes. So warm.

"The sheriff thinks so, but I don't," he replied with a shrug. "If I did, I wouldn't be here."

That was a relief. At least I had one cop on my side. "I'm not guilty."

"I know. You don't have the makeup of a killer, unless you're some type of psychopath, which I don't think you are."

Tears actually welled in my eyes as I glanced down at my coffee cup. Perhaps I was a psychopath, but I'd never admit it. No one else I knew talked to ghosts. "Thank you. I'm actually nervous being at the house alone."

"Because of your ghosts?"

I glanced over at Ruby and shook my head. "No. It just makes me scared to think someone could have come in while I was sleeping and killed Mr. Gonzalez. But you've helped to put my mind at ease. I appreciate it."

My phone rang and both of us looked at it. *Jumping Jack's Jeep Tours* came up on the screen. The only reason he'd be calling was to either tell me he had sent someone over to stay with me, or he needed to cancel our ride in the afternoon. "I need to take this."

"Sure. Go ahead."

I picked up my phone. "Hi, Jack."

"Hey. Listen, I need to reschedule our ride. I had another group come in for a tour."

"Of course." I certainly wasn't going to be upset about him filling his time with money-making clients. "You let me know when."

"Sounds good. Probably tomorrow. I'll talk to you later."

I hung up and smiled at Adam as I set down my phone.

"Are you two dating?" he asked. His question caught me off guard and I could only stare at him a moment. His cheeks reddened slightly, and he suddenly became even cuter. "Sorry, I don't mean to pry."

"No, I'm not dating Jack," I blurted, finally able to find my voice. "We're friends. That's it."

Adam nodded, then rose to his feet. "I better get back to work. But I was wondering if you'd be interested in maybe going out with me one day?"

I also stood and nodded, trying to play it cool when really I was a jumbling mess of nerves and excitement. "I'd like that," I said softly.

"Great," he said, smiling like I'd just made his morning. "Once this investigation is put to bed, I'll give you a call."

As he walked out the door, Ruby stared at me and shook her head. "Bernie, you don't date cops!"

"Mind your own business," I muttered.

"Excuse me?" The older woman sitting on the couch said, glaring at me over her glasses. "What did you say?"

"Sorry. Nothing. Just talking to myself."

Dang Ruby. I had to stop having conversations with her when others were around.

But, holy moly... Adam wanted to date me?

In the past, after Jack had introduced us, we'd said hello a few times in passing around town and ran into each other on the hiking trails. I'd always put my business first and really didn't want to date, but with Adam, I may just change my mind.

My outlook on life would have drastically improved... if I didn't have a murderer hanging around my peripheral vision.

CHAPTER 13

The next morning, I stood on the second floor of my house and stared out the window at the end of the hallway at the oh, so important car that someone didn't want me to go near which was still parked in my back lot. Why had they left it? Why didn't they come and get it? And more importantly, why hadn't the police taken it away? They obviously didn't know about it, and I couldn't tell them. My caller had made it clear if I did, I'd die.

All I wanted was for the darn car to disappear. My stomach twisted with unease and my chest actually ached from my nervousness. I'd been caught up in something I didn't understand and I hated the sudden turn my life had taken into chaos and the unknown.

I preferred my life orderly and predictable. Things had changed so dramatically after being hit by lightning. I could now see my ghost. I'd grown somewhat accustomed to having her around, but when I thought

119

about it, I wanted to run screaming from the building. Her being the exact opposite of me in personality also wore on my nerves. I loved her, but if I were being honest, she only added to my anxiety. Now I was also stuck in the middle of a murder investigation and I had to find a way out.

Speaking of orderly, my house was anything but. Although I had tried to ignore it for the most part and relax a little, I simply couldn't. I hated my things in disarray. I turned back to the guestrooms, deciding it was time to clean up the mess the police had left. Dismissing it any longer wasn't an option.

"Honey, you really need to take a chill pill," Ruby said as she appeared at the top of the stairs. Having a ghost materializing at the end of the hallway should absolutely freak me out, but it didn't. "The stress is pouring off you like a thick sludge. You're going to get wrinkles before your time."

I studied her features as I approached. Ruby had never had many wrinkles, her face always soft and smooth, except for the laugh lines that pinched as she smiled at me. I, on the other hand, possessed a worry crease between my brows that never seemed to dissipate, no matter how many creams and treatments I slathered on. "I'll feel better once the house is in order."

Ruby reached her hand out to me, and we both watched the ghostly fingers brush right through my arm as a chill traveled from my wrist and down my spine. "Honey, there's more to life than a clean house."

"I know that," I said gently as tears of helplessness

welled in my eyes. I wanted to be like her and forget it all, but I couldn't. "Right now, it's the only thing I can control, so I'd appreciate you allowing me some space to do what I need to in order to feel slightly better about everything instead of lecturing me on how uptight I am."

Her mouth opened in surprise, as if she wanted to say something. Finally, she just grinned. "Of course. But don't forget about our ATV ride this afternoon!" She faded away.

I spent the next few hours cleaning up the mess the cops had made, except for the room where Mr. Gonzalez had died. With most of my house finally in order, I felt much better about my life in general. Ruby had always insisted I had OCD—even when I was younger—which had also occurred to me more than a few times in my adult life. I hated disorganization and silly things like the towels not being stacked with the folds facing outward, half-filled salt and pepper shakers, or toilet paper rolls that fed from underneath instead of the top.

I also hung out my closed sign. Until I knew exactly what had happened in my house and who was responsible, I didn't want strangers coming and going.

Standing out in the hallway by the death room, as Ruby had called it, I stared at the closed door. Even though I lived with the dead, going into the bedroom where Mr. Gonzalez had died scared me just a bit. It shouldn't, but it did. I *slept* in the very room where Ruby had died and I never gave it a second thought.

Probably because I never believed in ghosts before moving in.

"He's not there," Ruby said. "He's gone to the other side. I already told you that. Lucky son of a—"

I pushed open the door half expecting Ruby to be wrong and for me to come face-to-face with a very angry spirit. If I had died from drinking a smoothie, I'd be very upset. However, I was met with another mess the cops had left and a blast of stale air.

They'd really done a number on the white and yellow room. Every single drawer had been pulled out and laid on the floor, the bed and nightstand shoved from the wall.

"You shouldn't move those by yourself," Ruby said. "You'll throw your back out. You should ask Jack to come help you."

I was thinking more along the lines of Adam, but she'd made it very clear she didn't approve of that potential relationship. "If I can't do it on my own, I'll call someone."

Satisfaction roiled through me when I finally got the bad back against the wall after a long struggle. Again, it was something I could control, and even though I had a line of sweat across my brow and a few pulled muscles in my back, I'd powered through and situated the furniture where it was supposed to be. A definite win in my day.

After everything was in its place and I'd made the bed, I stepped back into the hallway and shut the door.

"Is it time yet?" Ruby asked, appearing right next to me.

With a yelp, I jumped backward and hit my arm against the wall. "Ow!" I yelled, rubbing my elbow. "Don't sneak up on me like that!"

Ruby chuckled and shook her head. "Okay, I'll stop it. Just so you know, you're stealing one of the few joys I have left. Being dead is an absolute bummer."

I pulled out my phone and glanced at the clock. Jack hadn't called, so I assumed our scheduled ride was still on. Frankly, I'd rather have skipped it, but I'd promised Ruby and didn't want to disappoint her. "Yes, it's time," I muttered. "Let's go. And remember to please be quiet when we get there so I can concentrate on what he's saying to me and not make a complete fool of myself."

"Woohoo!" Ruby yelled in my ear as we followed Jack through town on the ATV. He sped along a little faster than I would have liked, but slower than Ruby would have preferred. "What's wrong with you two? Crank this baby up and let's see what it's got under the hood!"

"How about you be quiet so I don't crash?"

"I'll be fine if you do!"

Shaking my head, I realized sometimes she didn't quite understand that despite my helmet, I was still made of flesh and blood and could end up a street stain, while she couldn't. "*I* might not be fine if I crash."

Not that the thought of hurting herself would have stopped her from pushing limits while alive.

"Good point. Drive carefully. Take care of yourself, and I'll keep the old trap shut."

Finally.

The wind whipped across my cheeks as we left the main road and made our way up into the hills. I fell back a little bit more to allow Jack's cloud of red dust to settle so I didn't eat dirt. As the machine rumbled beneath me and we climbed the crimson mountain, I took in the desert beauty around me.

Towering red rocks spanned hundreds of feet up in the air. Little yellow sagebrush flowers, and beautiful Saguaro cacti stood on the sides of the trail, their bent arms seeming to wave at me. The sun shone in the blue sky above and warmed my bare arms.

Why didn't I do this more often?

"Hang on!" I yelled as I hit the gas. Ruby squealed in delight behind me. Glancing down, I saw her ghostly arms around my waist, yet her body reminded me of a cool pack as it rested against my back.

"Faster, Bernie!" she yelled in my ear, and I obliged.

I noted a place in the trail up ahead where I could overtake Jack, and I floored it. We flew over bumps in the terrain and I struggled to keep the ATV under my power, yet, I didn't want to slow down.

"Eat her dust, loser!" Ruby yelled as we passed Jack and headed up the steep hill.

When we reached the place where we could go either right or left, I pulled over and waited.

"You're crazy!" Jack said with a chuckle, coming to a stop beside me. "I thought you were going to crash!"

He wasn't the only one. I was one jerk of the handlebars from completely losing control and rolling down the hill in a mess of flesh and metal. And it had felt great. "Where to now?"

"I thought we'd head to the right," Jack said. "There's a really pretty view of town, and someone just cut the trail."

"Doesn't the parks department have to do that?" Ruby asked. "Not that I'm up on all park rules, but I thought it was their job."

"Good question," I said.

Jack stared at me, his brow furrowed in confusion. "I... I didn't ask you anything."

Dang it!

"Let's head to the right like you suggested," I said, ignoring his comment. Maybe if I pretended everything was fine and I didn't sound like a crazy person, he wouldn't question me about my other conversation.

Jack nodded and turned right. I followed at a distance, enjoying the vast desert scenery below us. Three years ago, when I'd discovered Ruby had willed me her house, I hadn't been certain I wanted to move from Louisiana to Arizona. I'd be leaving my family and starting fresh. That both scared and thrilled me, so I had decided to go west and stay for a month to get a feel for the town and area. Of course, I had great memories of being with Ruby during the summers I had stayed with her, but I had no doubt things would be different without her.

At first I had missed her so badly, I'd simply walked around the house and cried. But slowly, I began to meet people, really see the area from an adults' point of view, and fell in love with the desert, towering red rocks, and outdoor activities. Sedona quickly became my home.

"It's so pretty, isn't it?" Ruby said. "I've missed this so much."

"I don't come out here often enough," I replied as I came to a halt and turned off the engine, wanting to take in the view just for a few moments before catching up to Jack again. "It's so relaxing."

"You don't *do* anything, honey," Ruby said. "You're either cleaning up after a guest, working on the marketing for the next one, or fretting over something else. You should be proud of what you've built, but your life is passing you by. You need moments like this... moments that take your breath away."

A hawk screeched from above and the rumble of Jack's motor up ahead slowly faded. A light breeze caressed my cheeks. The stillness and quiet of the desert seemed unworldly and almost deafening.

Of course, she was right.

I stared at the vast expanse for another moment, then started the engine. The hum broke the silence and my moment of reflection. Perhaps I did need to save up and get my own ATV. I loved being out in the desert and riding until my heart raced.

When I parked behind Jack, I heard him curse as he bent over. I cut my motor and walked over to him.

"I hate when people leave their garbage around like this," he said, picking up a Sarah's Smoothie cup. "It really makes me mad."

Glancing around, I realized we'd literally driven to the end of a ledge. Ruby walked past me to the edge and then turned to me.

"Hey, Bernie!" she called. "Watch this!"

I screamed as she jumped.

CHAPTER 14

"*What?! What's wrong?*" Jack yelled as he glanced around, his eyes wide in fright.

Ruby appeared next to me in a fit of giggles as I dropped to my knees. "I'm dead, girl," she said. "And tethered to you. Remember? I'm not going anywhere."

"What's happening, Bernie?" Jack shouted once again.

"Nothing! I'm sorry. I shouldn't have screamed. I'm afraid of heights and didn't realize how high we'd come."

He stared at me for a moment, then sat next to me. "Are you okay? I thought you saw a rattlesnake or some other critter."

"No," I replied, then removed my helmet. "I'm okay. The ledge caught me off guard." Dang Ruby and her stupid jokes. She bounced around the edge and my heart thundered, but I turned to Jack and ignored her.

"I've never found garbage up here before," Jack said. "I was just here a couple of days ago."

Glancing around, I noted footprints and an indentation in the red dirt that looked like the outline of a human body. Who would come up here to take a nap? Talk about truly getting away from it all for a rest.

"I know you're afraid of heights, but you should look over the edge," Jack continued. "You can see Sedona and the desert for miles around. It's really pretty."

Standing, I walked over and looked. Yes, the whole town was visible, as was my house. I could clearly see the dirt lot out in back and my SUV sitting next to the black car I wasn't supposed to go near.

Had someone been lying in the dirt, watching my house? I slowly turned and glanced around, suddenly very uncomfortable and feeling like I was being watched.

Then I remembered Jack's dirty pants the day I'd gone in to rent the ATV. He'd said not too many people knew about this spot, and the trail had recently been cut. Had he been up here surveilling my house? Was he somehow involved in this murder?

"What's wrong?" Ruby asked. "You look like you just saw Satan himself."

And as I turned and smiled at Jack, perhaps I *was* staring directly at Satan himself. Why had Jack brought me out to the middle of nowhere, up onto this peak? To push me off and end my involvement in his scheme, never to be found again? Or was he letting me know that he was studying every move I made, and this was a non-verbal threat?

"You were right—this is nice," I said, moving against the wall of rock and taking a seat in the dirt. I'd be a lot harder to move as deadweight on the ground. "I'm glad we came up here."

"Me, too," he said, stretching out next to me. "I love the quiet. I can't believe someone else knows about this place and they actually leave their garbage here. That really gets me. What if an animal were to try to eat that cup? A bobcat or an elk? It could kill them."

With a nod, I tried to relax. If he was up to something nefarious, I couldn't let him know I was aware of it. I had to play it cool for a bit, then when we headed back, I'd leave him behind and find my way to safety.

Or maybe my imagination had gone into overdrive and he simply wanted to bring me up to see the magnificent view. I'd remain on guard but try to enjoy myself.

"Do you want some water?" he asked, reaching into his bag and pulling out two bottles.

Even though I was absolutely parched and my tongue felt like it had a layer of dirt coating it, I shook my head. If he was involved, he knew about the poison Mr. Gonzalez had ingested. What if he was trying to poison me and leave my body for the vultures? Nope. He wouldn't get me that easily. I'd go down with a fight and stay one step ahead of him.

"Water?" Ruby said, curling her lip in disgust. "I

would think a beer would be a far better way to celebrate such a magnificent view."

Jack talked for another half-hour about Las Vegas, Nevada, where he'd grown up. I didn't hear much of what he said because my mind was preoccupied with not being murdered. Well, that and watching Ruby dance around the edge of the drop-off like she didn't have a care in the world. She seemed absolutely clueless to my stress while my heart thundered, sweat formed on my brow despite the breeze, and I felt like I would vibrate right out of my skin at any moment.

I had to get off this ledge.

Part of me wanted to run down to the ATV, hop on, and speed away. However, if Jack was involved in the murder, I was afraid he'd overtake me and hurt or kill me.

"Have you ever been there?" Jack asked.

I hadn't heard the question. "No," I said, hoping he was asking about maybe the moon or Paris—somewhere far away and not some local joint that I most likely was very familiar with.

"Are you okay, Bernie?" he asked. "I feel like you're somewhere else."

Just attempting to stay alive and wondering how to get out of the situation.

"What's wrong with you?" Ruby asked, settling down on the other side of me. "You're acting like this handsome specimen of a man has a plan to kill you or something."

"He might," I said under my breath.

"Really?" she said, glaring at him. "Why do you think that?"

"Bernie?" Jack said. "Are you okay?"

I nodded and turned to him. "I've got a bit of a stomachache." And I wasn't lying. My stress levels had my stomach in knots while bile rose in my throat. If I didn't remove myself from the situation, I feared I might vomit.

"Should we leave right now?" he asked, his brow pinched in concern.

I grabbed my helmet. "I think that may be a good idea."

Both of us stood and he motioned for me to head down the pathway before him. I glanced at the trail and quickly decided I wouldn't be going first. He could push me over the ledge too easily if my back was to him. "You go ahead," I said. "I'll follow."

Jack shrugged and started down the hill.

"What's going on with you?" Ruby asked, but I ignored her as I carefully watched my footing and Jack while keeping a good fifteen feet away. I'd already decided I'd knock him in the head with my helmet if he even glanced at me strangely. "I wasn't ready to leave!"

"Race you back?" Jack asked, smiling as we reached the ATVs.

I slipped on my helmet but didn't lock the strap. If I needed to beat him with it, immediate access was crucial. "Sure."

He started up his ATV and took off. I sighed in relief as I straddled mine. "You probably didn't notice, but that ledge directly overlooked our house," I said. "There was an indentation in the dirt, as though someone had been lying down right there. And Jack did say the trail had recently been cut. What if he's involved? What if he brought me up here—"

"I get it, Bernie," Ruby said, her voice grave. "I didn't put it all together that you could be in danger. Let's ride, girl. Get you back to safety."

Finally, she understood.

We followed Jack for a half-mile, then he pulled over. I swore under my breath as I stopped about six feet away, still trying to maintain the façade of normalcy.

"You still up for that race?" he asked, his grin in place. At one time, I'd found it charming. Now, not so much. With the dimples, he gave the impression of a murderer in a pretty disguise, like most serial killers.

"Sure." *Act normal. Nothing is wrong.*

I figured we had about a mile left before we'd hit city streets. The trail was wide enough for both of us to ride, so we took off, neck and neck.

"The faster we get you back to civilization, the better off you'll be!" Ruby yelled into my ear.

I nodded and hit the gas, pulling ahead. Jack kept up. I felt like I was in a race for my life. Like he'd allow me to live if I won. A little dramatic, I know, but I'd become so worked up and convinced Jack had something to do with Mr. Gonzalez dying.

Jack approached, his ATV mere inches from my leg.

As I tried to veer to the left a little, he moved over again.

"Is this jerk trying to push you off the trail?" Ruby asked.

With my full concentration on controlling the machine beneath me, I couldn't answer. But yes, I would have to agree. If I moved off the trail now, I'd hit a cactus or brush and end up eating dirt.

"Slow down!" Ruby yelled. "Let him win!"

But I couldn't. If I slowed down, he still had me trapped out in the desert. As long as I kept moving toward town, he wouldn't be able to hurt me.

When he inched toward me again, I wondered if he was truly trying to run me off the trail in hopes of finishing me off or if he just wanted to claim victory.

The trail began to narrow and our ATVs drew closer together. We were headed for a crash, but I could also see the road that led to civilization and my safety. I focused on it and amped up the gas one more time.

Going way too fast, I pulled in front of Jack just as the trail narrowed further. There was nothing for him to do to win but to off-road, which would be dangerous with the shrubs and cacti.

"That's my girl," Ruby said as we pulled up to the main street leading back to town. "Way to show him who's boss."

I didn't bother to stop and gloat over my win, but instead drove into traffic, which garnered me a honk from the car I cut off.

Safety. Finally. I sighed and realized I'd been holding my breath. My heart still galloped and my hand ached from holding the handlebars so tightly, but at least I knew I would live to see another day.

However, I still had to play it cool with Jack when we returned to his business.

As I pulled into the parking lot, I glanced behind me and found him a couple of cars back. I forced a grin as he parked next to me.

"You're crazy!" he yelled with a chuckle. "I thought we were going to crash back there!"

"Thanks for taking me out today," I said, yanking off my helmet. "I appreciate it."

And I did, even though I'd felt my life was in danger. At least I could say I had a pretty good idea of the spot from where the killer watched my house.

"Sure! It was fun. I'm glad we did this. Are you feeling better?"

"A little. I think I just need to lay down for a while. Maybe take an antacid."

Just then, a car pulled in and four people emerged. They headed for the office.

"Duty calls," Jack said. "Can I take the helmet and keys and I'll go help those customers?"

I handed him both. "Thanks again, Jack."

He waved as he strolled over to the building and my shoulders sagged in relief. I'd made it out of the desert alive.

"Let's get out of here," I mumbled to Ruby.

"I don't think that's going to happen," she replied. "Looks like Darla has something to say to you."

Turning around, I found my friend marching toward me, a look of determination on her face.

"That is one unhappy lady there," Ruby said. "She's got words for you."

"What do you think you're doing?" Darla said, her cheeks crimson.

"I'm not sure what you mean," I replied. "What am I doing with what?"

"Are you dating him?"

"Who?"

"Jack!" Darla yelled. "Are you dating Jack?! Because I didn't think that's something you would do, but I never imagined you telling the police I could be a murderer either!"

"Wait a minute," I said, holding my hands up between us. "First, no, I'm not dating Jack. Second, I *had* to tell the police that you were in contact with Mr. Gonzalez."

"What are you doing with Jack then? Just out in the desert riding around?"

"Exactly. We're friends, Darla. You know that."

She crossed her arms over her chest and narrowed her gaze on me. "I thought we were friends. First you throw my name out to the police, and if you're trying to steal Jack from me, I swear..."

Well, hit me over the head with a two-by-four of shock. I had no idea Darla and Jack were dating. He'd always been the playboy of the town and I'd never known him to date anyone exclusively.

"No," I said. "I'm not seeing Jack and I have no interest in him whatsoever. But frankly, I'm surprised you do."

Darla stared at me for a moment, then turned on her heel and marched back to the diner.

I felt like I'd just walked into another dimension of my life, one I didn't fully understand where no one acted as they were supposed to. Darla and Jack? When had that happened? Before or after the murder?

"Looks like she was a sucker and fell for the dimples," Ruby said.

I nodded, wondering if my brain was about to explode. I needed to get back to my place to think things through, but I was absolutely parched from our ride and my own nerves.

What if Jack and Darla had been working together and *they* were the killers?

CHAPTER 15

On the way back to my house I stopped at the grocery store. I caught a glimpse of myself in the window and almost didn't recognize my reflection. My windblown hair hung in matted, crazy waves around my face, while my bangs had been plastered to my forehead. Red dirt covered me from head to toe. I definitely resembled a rat that had just crawled out of the desert.

I had wanted to immediately head home, but I needed food. My stomach howled with hunger and the sleeve of crackers in my pantry wasn't going to cut it. The police had taken almost everything from my refrigerator, not even leaving my soy milk for my coffee that morning. I needed a restock.

As I pushed my cart around, I sucked down a bottle of water. Ruby trailed behind me, surprisingly quiet. She didn't even hum. I glanced back a few times to make sure she was still with me, and she didn't meet my gaze. Something preoccupied her.

I stopped before turning down the cookie aisle. Ruby ghosted right through me, causing goosebumps to cascade over my skin. It didn't bother me as much as the two people I now stared at.

The Thompsons stood at the end of the aisle.

"Oh! Are we getting cookies?!" Ruby said excitedly. "I love chocolate chip!"

"Look," I whispered. "Didn't they say they were leaving town?"

Ruby glanced over. "Well, well, well. Liar one and Liar two continue their stampede of fabrications and falsehoods."

I narrowed my gaze on the couple. *"W-we've decided we don't feel safe here,"* Bobbie had said. *"We're going to leave town."*

So what were they doing here looking at cookies in the supermarket?

"Get closer and I'll see if I can hear what they're saying," Ruby said. "Keep your back to them and they won't notice you."

I pushed the cart toward them as instructed while Ruby walked ahead. When she'd reached the end of the connection we shared, she was forced to take a few steps back. I stopped about fifteen feet away, which put Ruby right behind them. Turning around, I studied the assortment of chocolate chip choices. The ones with marshmallows and nuts looked particularly tasty, so I grabbed two packages. Stress and my grandmother's bad habits had me making all sorts of poor decisions.

Moments later, the Thompsons walked off without noticing me and Ruby sauntered over.

"Oh, those are good!" she said, glancing in my cart. "I did prefer the ones without the nuts, though. You may like them better."

"What did they say?" I whispered, putting one of the packages back and grabbing the one without nuts.

"Well, they enjoy lemon cookies, which explains why I didn't like them. Rule four-hundred-and fifty-two of life: People who like lemon cookies aren't to be trusted."

"Why is that?"

"I don't know," Ruby said with a shrug. "I've never met anyone decent who likes them. It's really quite a strange thing. For instance, I found out during our brief dating stint that Sheriff Walker can eat them by the dozen. He's as close to a dictator as you can get."

I rolled my eyes. "He's not that bad. He just didn't want you partaking in things that were illegal."

Ruby shrugged and crossed her arms over her chest. "I don't appreciate people telling me what to do."

"What did the Thompsons say?" I whispered, hoping to get the conversation back on track.

"That they'd get the package tomorrow, and then they'd leave town."

Interesting. But what did it mean?

"Did they elaborate on what they were getting?"

"Nope. Just what I said and then they debated on

whether to get two boxes of lemon cookies or just one, but Bobbie said the cookies would give her gas, so they should only get the smaller box."

I ignored the information on Bobbie's gastro-intestinal issues and considered the rest of the conversation.

The package could refer to anything—a specialized set of essential oils from Elizabeth's Essentials, some custom-made cowboy boots from Boots n' Bags, a handcrafted piece of jewelry... or something else. Maybe the car parked in back of my place? Or whatever was in the car? Perhaps they used the term package instead of car in case anyone overheard them?

The two had been lying from the start. They'd never gone hiking or practiced yoga out at Cathedral Rock, and they'd never left town.

Perhaps they had been responsible for Mr. Gonzalez's death, checked in like they'd never been inside my house to keep an eye on the car, and then when the police came, they scattered, afraid their involvement would be discovered.

I continued up the cookie aisle, ruminating. After a moment, I found myself in the wine section.

"Get a nice red to go with the cookies," Ruby said. "Is there anything better a pairing of chocolate and red wine?"

It had been so long since I had any sugar, I couldn't agree or disagree. Instead, I trusted her judgment and grabbed a bottle of Cabernet. If anyone knew cookies and wine, it was Ruby. Or in her case, probably cookies and tequila. Or bourbon. Or beer. I couldn't imagine her being picky on which alcohol to consume.

As I set the bottle in my cart, I glanced up to see one of the stockers staring at me. Probably making sure I wasn't stealing anything. In my current state, I could definitely be labeled as suspicious. But in the vegetable aisle, a couple of locals glared at me as if I'd somehow wronged them.

"Why is everyone staring at me?" I whispered as I grabbed a bag of spinach.

"Well, you do look like something dead a bobcat dragged in from the desert," Ruby said. "Saying you appear a little rough around the edges right now is being kind."

"I was busy running for my life," I grumbled, trying to run my fingers through my hair.

"You *think* you were running for your life, Bernie. At no time were you threatened, either physically or verbally. You obviously get your flair for the dramatics from me."

Had I been in danger with Jack? The more time I put between me and the situation, the more confused I became. Had I been seeing clues that weren't there?

"My goodness," Ruby said with a chuckle. "Listen to me... the voice of reason. That doesn't happen very often."

Had my whole encounter with Jack and the fact I could see my house from the ledge been nothing but a big coincidence?

I nodded in agreement at Ruby's statement. She was

right on that one. In fact, it turned out she was right about a lot of things. I returned to the wine aisle and grabbed another bottle.

In the dairy section, I found Stan from As the Pins Drop whispering heatedly with Sarah from the smoothie place.

"Let's get closer," Ruby said. "I'm kind of digging this eavesdropping business you've got me doing."

As I pushed my cart toward them, Ruby walked out in front me once again. She motioned to me as she reached the end of our tether. Stan reached out and clasped Sarah's shoulder, then leaned over and kissed her cheek. My goodness—they argued like snakes one moment, then a gentle, loving kiss? What was their relationship, and what were they disagreeing about? I inched closer, hoping to appear as inconspicuous as possible, but unfortunately, Sarah saw me before Ruby could get within hearing distance.

She elbowed Stan and the three of us stared each other down. With a smile, I waved at them, hoping to appear friendly despite my dragged-from-the-gutter look.

"What happened to you?" Sarah asked, studying me from head to toe and not bothering to try to hide her discontent.

"ATV ride," I said.

"A rough one," Sarah agreed with a snort.

"Yes," I replied, running my hand over my hair once again. "Everything okay?"

"Sure," Stan said, his voice harsh and letting me

know things were definitely not okay. "You got a lot of nerve talking to either one of us, though."

"Why is that?" I asked, my heart slowly sinking, my smile fading.

"You gave my name to the police," Stan spat. "They came in and were all up in my business. Sheriff Walker said I had you to thank for that."

Typical Arizonian—no one wanted anyone else in their business, and I felt the same. I probably wouldn't have thrown out anyone's name if I didn't have some creepy caller watching me, threatening my life and telling me how to keep breathing.

"They asked who Mr. Gonzalez came in contact with while in town. Do you want me to lie to the police, Stan?"

"I want to live my life," Stan mumbled, some of his bluster gone.

"As do I, but a man died in my house, and unfortunately, you had a disagreement with him. I'm sorry I inconvenienced you by including your name."

"You tell him, Bernie," Ruby said, standing next to me. "And also let him know his dad was a bad kisser."

I pinched my lips together and shook my head. "I'll see you both some other time." After rounding the corner, I turned to Ruby. "Everyone hates me!"

"They'll get over it," she said, waving her hand between us. "Time makes people forget."

"What do you mean?"

"Well, I grew up in a pretty strict Catholic family. We had Sunday mass, went to confession once a week, and also attended catechism. When I was bad, my father whooped me with a switch he cut from the backyard willow tree. One day, I finally poured bleach on the darn thing so it died."

I cringed at the thought of being abused like Ruby had been.

"It was a different time, and I wasn't having any of it —like I'd been born too early. I couldn't fit the mold of what they thought a child should be. My mother would fret, worried that Dad would get home and dinner wouldn't be ready. Her whole world centered around him. I was the child that was seen as long as my dress was pressed and my curls hung right around my cheeks and I kept my mouth shut. I was told I was pretty or that I danced well. I don't think they ever referred to me as smart.

"Anyway, as I grew up, I was determined to be heard. Everyone would listen to me, everyone would see me, and it didn't matter what my dress or hair looked like. By the time I was eighteen, I was on my own. The black sheep of the family, who my parents had all but disowned. My extended family were horribly embarrassed for them. I mean, I had a child out of wedlock! And I wasn't sure who the father was. Back then, that was a one-way ticket to hell, according to my parents and relatives. But they all started coming out of the woodwork once I began to make money from my psychic business. It seemed everyone grew to love me then. In time, they forgot about the horrid wild-child and instead, wanted something from me. It's a little different from your situation right now, but people forget."

"That's really sad," I murmured. "We need to talk about it more."

"We really don't," Ruby said with a laugh. "Just remember that most people don't carry grudges forever. Life rule number one-hundred-and-ninety-six. All this nonsense will blow over before you know it. If I can gain the respect of my family after being such a horrible disappointment to them, you'll regain the trust of all these idiots in this town."

I wiped my brewing tears, grabbed a couple other items, and headed for the cashier. "Oh, pick up that rag," Ruby said, pointing at the celebrity gossip magazine rack. "Let's read about the royals."

After opening up to the article, I lost myself in it while Ruby read along with me.

"I didn't know they did that. Did you?" Ruby asked. "My goodness."

"Right?" I whispered. "I don't think I'd want to be a royal."

"Oh, I would," Ruby said. "You can basically do anything you want and no one cares."

"What are you talking about? They have so many rules! Their lives are very stringent."

"Well, I guess you're right," she replied. "I'd probably get kicked out. Be the black sheep of the royal family." Her mouth turned in a frown. "I guess I was already a black sheep. We didn't wear crowns, though."

We stared at each other for a moment, and just then

the woman behind me cleared her throat. I glanced up to find it was my turn to empty my cart onto the conveyor belt.

I had just unloaded my wine and spinach when I noticed movement out of the corner of my eye toward the front of the store.

Four policemen, one of them being Adam, had walked in. For a brief second, I marveled at how good looking he was, until he strode right to me. With a gasp, I pushed my cart between them and me. I hadn't touched Mr. Gonzalez, and I wouldn't go down without a fight.

One of the cops drew his gun and gripped it at his side. Another held his taser at the ready. Oh, wow. They weren't messing around. My bluster fizzled out of me faster than false news traveled on social media.

"Hold it right there," one cop said.

"You're under arrest!" Adam yelled. "Get on the floor!"

CHAPTER 16

*T*he cops hadn't been after me. Instead, they'd had their sights on the checker who was ringing up my groceries, a man in his early twenties I didn't know. That being said, I'd about fainted when they rushed toward the checkout stand and Adam had met my gaze for a brief moment. I'd thought they'd found something to implicate me in the murder, then wondered who had set me up.

I had never been so thankful to be so wrong.

Once they'd hauled away the checker, someone else had stepped in and bagged up my groceries. I paid with trembling hands as I listened to the whispers and gossip around me. After eavesdropping for just a few moments, it became apparent no one had any idea what the young employee had done.

With too much to haul home on my own, I stole the shopping cart and pushed it down the sidewalk, sending Ruby into fits of giggles.

"With the cart, you do look homeless," she said, gasping. "Why don't you pop open a bottle of wine and complete the picture?"

"Homelessness isn't funny," I muttered.

"Oh, honey, I've been there and done that. Nothing funny about it. Just knowing you and your panache for perfection... at the moment, you don't look like you. It's like I've entered another facet of reality to find you in this state. That's the funny part."

Ignoring her, I stopped at Sarah's Sensational Smoothies as my mood continued its downward spiral. It had definitely not been my day.

Thankfully, Sarah wasn't there. The last thing I needed was to suffer under her nasty glare once again. I retrieved my smoothie without any further altercations.

When Ruby and I finally arrived home, I immediately headed for the shower and made a mental note to return the shopping cart the next day. The red dirt that had been in my hair and covering my skin swirled down the drain, the coloring reminding me of blood, and I couldn't help but wonder if I'd almost lost my life that afternoon. Had Jack taken me up to that ledge to kill me, to warn me he had his eye on me, or had it all been a coincidence?

Despite the hot water, a chill ran down my spine.

And what the heck was up with Darla? We'd spent hours discussing Jack's wandering eye and lack of commitment in relationships. He was a nice guy and I did like him as a friend, but when had Darla crossed over that friendship zone and into a relationship?

"Hurry up, Bernie," Ruby said from the other side of the curtain. "We've got to figure out this murder right now."

"Could I please have some privacy?" I said, instinctively crossing my arms over my bare chest. Boundaries had never been Ruby's strong suit.

"Just hurry up. I have an idea."

I shut off the water and stepped out of the tub to get dressed. My stomach growled with hunger, which only reminded me I needed to eat at some point. Thankfully, I had purchased a large smoothie from Sarah's and still had some left over.

After drying my hair, I ventured out into the living room looking for my ghost. I found her on the sofa with Elvira curled at her side, the feline purring loudly. Before my life had drastically changed and I couldn't see Ruby, I would have thought I simply had a very happy cat, that my presence alone caused her to rumble like an engine—not that she actually loved to curl up next to my dead grandmother.

"Took you long enough," Ruby grumbled. "Sit, girl. We need to get this mess figured out."

As she pointed to the couch across from her, I realized I'd never seen her so serious. I sat down and waited, slowly sipping my peanut butter and chocolate smoothie piled high with whipped cream.

"Your ride with Mr. Dimples made you think your life was in danger today, and that really bothers me," she said. "We need to figure out who the killer is so that you can feel safe and able to get back to living instead of worrying."

I didn't bother to mention I was a perpetual worrier with or without a murder hanging over my head.

"Therefore," she continued, "and I never thought I would say this, but I think we need to go to the police." I waited for her to burst out laughing, but she only stared me down.

"You're serious?"

"More serious than the heart attack that killed me," Ruby claimed.

Setting my cup to the side, I nodded and wished my cat liked me more than my dead grandmother. Elvira hadn't even looked up when I came into the room, perfectly content with sitting next to Ruby. Traitorous feline. "What am I supposed to tell them? That I lied because my ghost told me to? That I also lied to them about the car out back? That I keep getting weird phone calls about the car, and I feel like everyone I know is part of it?"

"That's a start."

"Ruby, they'll haul me off to the funny farm!"

"Or they'll appreciate you helping them out to find the killer."

"How would I have done that?"

"Well, we now know from where these people are watching the house. We also know there are three main suspects who came in contact with Gonzalez before he died: Stan, Darla, and Sarah. And let's throw Jack in there as well since he's dating darling Darla and you felt threatened by him. One of them—or maybe two—has to be the killer. Unless you did it, of course."

"That's what the cops think."

"We don't know that for sure. They may just be covering their bases. Adam already told you he doesn't think you're guilty."

I stared at her a moment, frankly surprised by how sensible she was being, and once again I wondered if I was hallucinating Ruby. Using her name and 'sensible' in the same sentence was like saying good decisions and alcohol belonged together.

But how could I possibly go to the police and tell them about my ghost without sounding nuttier than a five-pound fruitcake?

"You know more about this case than they do," Ruby continued. "Heck, you could probably solve it yourself if you knew what was in that car!"

She was right. The car was the key to it all, and if I could discover what was in it, I might be able to tell the police who was responsible for the murders. But honestly, what would the evidence inside the car look like? A note that said, this package is for <insert murder suspect name>?

And if I did approach the vehicle again, what if someone tried to kill me—as they said they would do—if I went near it?

I could do nothing and just let the whole process play out. But again, I was still a suspect, and I would prefer to take control and prove my innocence.

"You know, I've been tossing around an idea about this car," I said.

"What's that?"

"Well, I agree with you that we need to find out what's inside."

"Smart girl," Ruby said, smiling and nodding. "Thinking like your old grandma. What are you going to do?"

I picked up my calorie and fat laden smoothie and took a long sip while I eyed Ruby and Elvira.

"You're going to help me."

"How am I going to do that?" Ruby asked, her ghostly face contorted in confusion. "In case you forgot, I'm dead."

"Well then, listen up, dead woman."

TWO HOURS AGO, I'd shut out all the lights and drawn the drapes just as I would while going to bed. Ruby and I sat in the dark in my bedroom and listened to the quiet of the night until it was time to move. Elvira was even more upset with me than before because I hadn't slipped under the covers with her. So she'd claimed my pillow and eyed me with blatant hatred. I fully expected a furball on my comforter sometime in the early morning hours.

When the clock struck midnight, we tip-toed to the back door. My hands trembled with nervous energy and Ruby shook her head. "I don't think I like this," she mumbled for the umpteenth time.

"It's going to be fine," I whispered.

"If everything is okay, why are you whispering?"

"I... I don't know."

Keeping my gaze on the car, I slowly opened the back door, slipped through, shut it and dropped to my stomach.

"You remind me of Rambo slithering across the lot like that," Ruby said, walking next to me.

I kept quiet, wishing I had the confidence Rambo possessed. Instead, I was the first to admit I was completely out of my element.

My plan had been for me to commando-crawl close enough to the car so Ruby could slip inside and see what it contained. With our tether, I had to be about fifteen feet from the vehicle. She hummed softly at my side as we slowly made our way across the dirt.

"Is it cool out?" she asked me. "It seems like there would be a slight chill in the air at this time of year."

Continuing my slow journey, I didn't answer and hoped she would quiet down. I needed to be able to hear everything around me. In the event someone approached and fulfilled their promise of killing me if I went near the car, I'd like to be aware they were coming and give myself a fighting chance of escaping—hopefully alive.

When I reached the back bumper of my SUV, I motioned for Ruby to enter the other vehicle that held all the secrets. She slipped through the back door, but I couldn't see anything with the tinted windows in the dark. I shut my eyes for a moment and listened to the surrounding area. A coyote howled in the distance, and the brush rustled as a brief breezed picked up. No footsteps, though, and I sighed in relief.

I imagined someone on the perch we'd visited staring down at my property with night-vision glasses, diligently watching the car. If that were the case, he'd have seen me crawl across the parking lot, my heat signature lighting up like a dang Christmas tree. It had been a risk for me to put my plan into action, but I had to save myself because my tormentors hadn't promised they *wouldn't* kill me once they retrieved whatever they were after in the car. Not that I'd believe them. In fact, I'd come to the conclusion that I would be dead whether they recovered the car or not.

A moment later, Ruby emerged.

"What did you find?" I whispered as she bent over me.

"Nothing."

I gritted my teeth and shook my head. How could that be? They'd made such a big deal about the stupid car; how could it contain absolutely nothing? "It's not the time for games, Ruby!"

She stood upright and placed her hands on her hips. "I'm not playing any games. There's nothing in the dang car, Smarty Pants."

"How can there be nothing in the car when I've had my life threatened multiple times over it?"

"I don't know. It's a head-scratcher, that's for sure."

While staring up at my bumper, I tried to figure out the mystery. Why was someone trying to scare me to death if there wasn't anything in the car? Why had Mr. Gonzalez been murdered? "Go look again," I whispered. "There has to be something you aren't seeing."

"There very well could be, but unfortunately, I can't move inanimate objects. I can't open the glove compartment or the catch-all between the seats."

Right. That little detail had escaped me.

"I looked inside the best I could, but I didn't see anything that screamed trouble."

"Is the car clean?" I asked.

"Very much so, except for the fast food bag on the back seat."

"Fast food?"

"Yes. It's crumpled up like he'd finished with it and tossed it on the floor behind his seat." Ruby glanced up at the sky and grinned. "Gosh, it's so pretty out here. The stars are so bright and the moon is starting to peek over the—"

She stilled for a moment, then ducked down. Her gaze met mine and panic gripped my chest.

"What is it?" I hissed.

Ruby placed her finger to her lips, motioning me to be quiet, then stood and walked toward the side of the house. I didn't know whether to stay where I was or find a place to hide. After listening intently, I thought I heard footsteps, but couldn't see anyone or anything except Ruby's ghostly feet standing about fifteen feet away. She tried to move farther toward the house, but our tether held her in place.

Slowly, I shimmied under my SUV, my breath coming in short spurts when the dirt crackled beneath me sounding louder than a cannon. As I stared up at the underbelly of my vehicle, it seemed to be sinking down on me, the space growing tighter by the second. Beads of sweat dotted my brow while more panic set in.

Ruby didn't return for what seemed like hours, but in reality, only a minute or two had passed. She hustled over, then dropped to her knees.

"Move!" she yelled and crawled under the car next to me as I inched over.

"What's going on?" I hissed. "Why are you hiding? No one can see you!"

"Shh! Someone's coming!"

CHAPTER 17

he fight or flight response is a funny experience, and definitely not the *ha-ha* kind. I debated whether to remain hidden, hoping I wasn't a sitting duck, or to roll out from under the car and run into either the house or out into the desert, which could give away my hiding spot. It was as if my mind were being ripped in two, leaving me paralyzed and unable to make a choice.

I had to think logically.

Had anyone seen me come out to the car?

That was the million-dollar question, for which I had no answer.

If yes, I needed to move. If no, I would be safe. But really, who would be out walking around at midnight in my back lot where the mysterious car had been parked? No one with good intentions, that's who. Someone who needed to protect the car and also wanted me dead since I'd violated their orders to stay away.

"Who is it?" I whispered.

"Not sure," Ruby said, the aroma of pot and lavender engulfing me because she was almost on top of me. "There's definitely footsteps, though. Whether they come into the lot or not remains to be seen."

I shut my eyes and listened to my surroundings. After a few moments, I turned to Ruby. "Are you sure someone's coming? I don't hear anything."

"Yeah, maybe I was wrong. I thought they'd have made an appearance by now."

I glanced again toward the side of the house where she'd thought she'd heard someone coming. Nothing. Maybe I was safe.

"Let's go back inside," Ruby said. "This was a bad idea, Bernie. Way too dangerous. I never should have let you talk me into this."

I didn't bother to remind her she'd been on board and actually excited about our clandestine operation an hour ago.

But was I ready to be out in the open? No. In fact, I was terrified to crawl out from under the car and back to my kitchen. Still, I couldn't stay under the car all night, either.

Or maybe I could. My limbs seemed to be locked up, frozen by fear.

"I don't know what to do," I mumbled, rubbing my eyes with my hands while pebbles dug into the back of my skull. The smell of tires and oil had incited a headache.

"Get out of here," Ruby said, moving out from under the car. "Let's go. The decision has been made. No one is here."

I slid out between my vehicle and Mr. Gonzalez's, remaining on my hands and knees for a few moments, sucking in fresh air. I felt safe hidden between the two cars, so I took a moment to gather my wits about me. Thankfully, my headache began to clear and my heart-beat calmed slightly. I didn't dare touch the offending car, but I did briefly consider breaking a window and taking a look inside myself to attempt to find what Ruby had missed—an idea I dismissed pretty quickly. Ruby was right. My plan had been a horrible one, and I wouldn't make any further bad decisions.

Eyeing the back door to my house, it looked to be a million miles away, but once inside, I intended to crawl under the covers and not emerge for a good twelve hours. Maybe more. The stress had eaten away all my energy.

Ruby let out a scream that would have peeled paint and I glanced up to find a figure come into view and stand between me and my house. I couldn't make out any features in the night, but by the bulk, it looked to be a man.

"Run, Rambo!" Ruby yelled. "We've failed our mission. Abort! Abort!"

I struggled to my feet and took off into the desert with Ruby literally floating behind me at the end of our connection. My chest had constricted from fear, but the adrenaline coursing through my body pushed me on as I jumped over brush and dodged cacti. I'd never been so happy for my dedication to physical fitness.

Glancing over my shoulder, I didn't see anyone chasing me, but I didn't stop to verify. I sprinted until my legs hurt not only from the exertion, but from the cacti and brush tearing at my leggings.

"You can stop," Ruby said from behind me. "He's not coming."

I dropped to my knees as my breath sawed in and out.

"Watch out for scorpions," Ruby muttered. "That's the last thing you need right now."

Tears streamed down my face as I hyperventilated. I kept checking over my shoulder, but I didn't see or hear anything strange.

"I think you lost him," Ruby said. "If I were him, I wouldn't have chased you all the way out here, no matter how bad I wanted to kill you."

After a few minutes, I rose to my feet. "Did you see who that was?"

She shook her head. "No. It's like he materialized out of nowhere."

"That was strange," I whispered. "I didn't even hear his footsteps."

"Me neither." She began pacing back and forth as far as our tether would allow. "You want to know who learns to walk silently?"

"The military?" I replied, shrugging.

"Also hunters."

"Who do we know that is involved in this who is a hunter or in the military?"

"Well, Jack had that deer head on his wall."

Placing my hands on my hips, I stared at the way I'd come. "And Stan had the military medals in that case at the bowling alley."

"Dancers also walk quietly," Ruby mused. "And so do ghosts. You're pretty light on your feet yourself."

My legs felt like lead after pounding my way through the desert. "Do you think Thompson is a dancer? He's tall and bulky."

"Maybe he's retired," Ruby said with a shrug. "He fattened himself up a bit."

It was a possibility. "How far do you think I ran?"

"I don't know. At least a mile. We've got a long trek home."

"I'm so tired, Ruby." I rubbed my hands over my jacket. Between my run and fumbling under the car, it had been ripped, along with my leggings.

"Let's get you home and to bed," Ruby said.

"I'm afraid to go back to the house, especially in the dark."

"What do you want to do? Sit out here the rest of the night?"

"I... I'm not sure what to do."

Ruby sighed. "Look, Bernie. We can't stay out in the middle of the desert all night. That may be even more dangerous than that guy. What if a psycho javelina finds you? They can be mean and give you a run for your money. Trust me. I've had a psycho javelina chase me, and a colonoscopy is slightly more enjoyable. Then there's the coyotes..."

Admittingly, I was curious about the story that included the javelina, but more pressing things needed to be dealt with.

"You're right. I need to head back." No matter how frightening the thought was, Ruby was right about this being worse.

We walked home, my ghost humming at my side. I needed to get my mind off my potential attacker, so I decided to focus on the past. "Tell me what happened after you had my mom."

I knew my mom, named Janis after Janis Joplin, had gone to live with my great-grandparents, but I didn't know the details and had never heard Ruby's side. Why not drudge up some family drama to keep my mind occupied?

"Well, my parents decided that I wasn't a fit mother, and maybe they were right, maybe they weren't. I didn't feel I was given a chance to prove I could be. They just took her. They could do stuff like that back then, especially with me being an unmarried sinner."

"And they went to Louisiana?"

"Yup. I think they just wanted to take her away from me. That was when she was a teen, so we had a bit of a relationship even though they convinced her I was a terrible mother."

I tried to imagine being in Ruby's shoes, and my heart ached for her. To have a child ripped away from me would devastate me.

"I worked hard to keep my relationship with Janis, and we did okay. When you came along, I was so excited to build a bond with you," she continued. "Thankfully, Janis allowed that by sending you out to live with me for the summers. I think she realized it would do you good. She's so darn uptight, just like my parents, but at least she has the sense to be aware of it."

Her description of my mother wasn't wrong. That was where I'd gotten my own idiosyncrasies from—my need for a neat and tidy house, my OCD, and my intense focus on my health. My mom had always worried I'd become heavy and instilled her fears in me. That had resulted in my singlemindedness regarding exercise and making healthy eating choices. I could probably call myself obsessed, and if I was honest with myself, it wasn't healthy in the least bit.

But Ruby seemed to be changing that for me because I was craving one of those peanut butter and chocolate smoothies, even though I'd just finished one that afternoon. I'd lived in Sedona for three years and I'd never even thought about consuming one.

"I wish I would have come to visit after I turned eighteen."

"Me, too, but don't get too worked up over it. I know you were just trying to live on the straight and narrow path you'd been brought up on."

Right again. I did a stint in college, became a yoga instructor and looking back, I wondered where my life would have gone if Ruby hadn't left me her house. Leaving Louisiana had been the best thing for me because I was out on my own and I had to make things work. I had no one to rely on like I did back home.

When I located the house in the distance, I hunched over and slowly walked the rest of the way, listening for any sound that seemed out of place. Unfortunately, I had never hunted nor had I been in the military, so each step seemed louder than a rocket launcher. I fumbled with my housekey and jammed it in the lock. I then hurried inside, shut the door and flipped the lock. Ruby ghosted through a moment later.

"That was rude," she said. "I'm certain your mom raised you not to slam the door in people's faces."

"Sorry," I said with a long exhale. "I wasn't thinking."

"That's okay, honey. You've got a lot on your plate right now."

Wasn't that the truth. I never imagined I'd find myself embroiled in a murder or seeing the dead.

"Can you please go check the rest of the house?" I asked. "Just to make sure no one is here?"

Ruby furrowed her brow and crossed her arms over her chest. "I thought you locked the doors."

"I did. But I'd appreciate you doing a quick check. What if that guy broke in? Maybe through a window up front? Or maybe picked the lock?"

"Ah, gotcha. Yes, ma'am. Be back in a flash."

I sat down with my back against the door and waited, closing my eyes and once again listening as hard as I could. The house sounded empty to me—no creaking floorboards, the low hum of televisions, or muffled voices I'd usually hear when I had guests. However, if someone had broken in and was waiting for the opportunity to do me harm, they wouldn't be walking around or watching TV. No, they'd be hidden, waiting for the right time to strike.

Thankfully, I had my ghost who could look in every nook and cranny for my potential attacker.

Ruby appeared about ten minutes later, just as I began to wonder if she'd forgotten about me. "No one else is in the house," she said.

"Did you check the closets?"

"Yes."

"Under the beds?"

"Yes."

"In every room?"

"For the love of the Grateful Dead, Bernie, yes! Do you think I'm going to risk someone being in this house and hurting you?"

"No," I said, my voice weak. "I just know that sometimes you cut corners with things."

"Sometimes, but not with my granddaughter's life. Geez." We stared at each other a moment and she shook her head. "No one is here."

"Okay, good," I said, standing. "Thanks for doing that and I'm sorry I questioned you."

"Of course. But there is one thing you aren't going to like."

"What's that?"

"Elvira left a hairball on your pillow."

CHAPTER 18

I slept a few hours, but had horrible nightmares, so it was like I didn't rest at all, feeling like I'd run another ten miles. With a groan, I rolled out of bed, more aware than ever that I needed help.

"Oh, good, you're up," Ruby said from the rocking chair where my barfy cat lay in the middle of her ghostly form. "Call Adam."

With a nod, I reached for my phone, then went to the kitchen to brew some coffee. Thank goodness I'd hung out my closed sign because I simply couldn't deal with new guests. The thought of having to greet others with a smile was simply asking too much. I needed the money, but I had to put my life back in order before opening again. Emotionally, I was a terrified wreck.

Adam answered on the second ring.

"Bernie?"

"I need to meet with you today," I blurted. "What time works for you?"

"What about?"

"The murder. Please, Adam. I need to talk to you about the murder."

"Okay, well, why don't you come down to the station and—"

"No. I'll meet you at the coffee shop."

He hesitated so long, I wondered if he'd hung up. "Um, okay."

"Half hour," I said, then ended the call.

"How are you going to pull yourself together and get over there in a half hour?" Ruby asked as I slugged down some coffee.

"I'm not pulling myself together," I grumbled.

Returning to my bedroom, I pulled on some track pants, sneakers and a sweatshirt. I didn't bother looking in the mirror because I knew what I'd find: matted hair, a scratched-up face, and half-crazed, exhausted eyes.

"I need you to stay here," I said, making my way back to the kitchen where Ruby had planted herself on the counter by the sink.

"Why is that?"

"I need to concentrate when I talk to him, and you make that very difficult." I poured more coffee, expecting her to argue. When she didn't, I turned to her.

"Fine," she replied, raising her chin and glaring at

me just enough for me to know it wasn't. "I'll be here with Elvira."

"Thank you," I whispered. "I appreciate your understanding."

"I'll head back to my tunnel for now... where I'm wanted," she said with a huff, slowly fading away.

I sighed in relief, thankful she wasn't in the mood to quarrel because I certainly wasn't. I was beyond exhausted and running on nothing but fumes and a little caffeine.

After sucking down another cup of coffee, I headed out the front door and hurried to Canyon Coffee. I had really wanted to drive, but I wouldn't even walk out my back door until the murder had been solved and that stupid car was off my property.

I arrived a few minutes before Adam and ordered him one of the strawberry custard treats I'd had last time. My stomach was too upset from the night's happenings to eat, so I took our coffee and his food to a couch and sat down, hoping I didn't fall asleep. The tension in my shoulders began to fade, and I realized I felt much safer out in public than I did at home, which was troublesome.

"It shouldn't be this way," I muttered, my anger flaring. I glanced down at my mood ring and found it red. At least it still worked correctly and hadn't been damaged in my frantic run the previous night.

I smiled when Adam entered and he took a seat next to me, his blue eyes glittering as he grinned, but then his smile faded. "What's up, Bernie? What happened to you?"

"I need help," I said, not bothering with formalities.

"With what?"

"I've lied," I blurted. "I've lied to you from the beginning and I can't do this anymore. Someone is trying to kill me and—"

"Whoa, hold up. Someone is trying to kill you?"

"Yes. Last night I—"

"Bernie, let's start at the beginning, okay?"

He placed his palm over my fingers. For some reason, the gesture brought tears to my eyes and I couldn't take my gaze from his strong hand. I trusted him. He cared. I felt it in the warmth of his touch, and finally, I was going to unburden myself to someone who could help. He gently squeezed and after a moment, I met his stare. All I needed to do was convince him I wasn't crazy and that Ruby did exist.

But what if she didn't? What if she was some figment of my imagination brought on by the lightning strike?

"Tell me what happened," Adam urged. "It's okay. You're obviously scared, but you don't need to be. I'm here to help."

The beginning. Where did that start?

Probably Louisiana.

"When I went back to Louisiana for my cousin's wedding, I was hit by lightning." I left out the part about the Voodoo ceremony. "After I got home, I realized something had changed."

"What was that?"

Here we go. "I have a ghost in my house. It's my dead grandmother, Ruby."

Adam stilled and raised an eyebrow. He stared at me a long moment, and his eyes flickered in confusion and indecision. Was I an Ace short of a full deck? I needed to press on.

"When Mr. Gonzalez was murdered, she told me to lie about it because she was the one who found him. I couldn't say that my dead grandmother's ghost discovered the body and came to tell me about it."

Adam nodded, as if everything I was saying made perfect sense.

"Then you started asking questions about how I found him. Ruby had me tell the story about the guest wanting me to wake him from the nap, but I wasn't home when he arrived. Darla Darling checked him in and I never saw him alive. I told the sheriff about that."

"Huh. Okay."

"But it gets worse," I said, taking a long sip of my coffee. "Much worse."

"Go on."

"Well, I realized I was a suspect and decided to solve the case. I told you all of this, but Stan from As the Pins Drop got into a fight with Gonzalez about his driving. Before Mr. Gonzalez checked in, he went to Sarah's Sensational Smoothies, and the poison was in the cup. Then this couple showed up at my house... the Thompsons. They lied to me about everything and we overheard them in the grocery store saying they were going to pick up the package and leave town."

"What package?"

"I'm getting to that."

"Okay, go on."

I took a deep breath and tried to order my thoughts. It was pointless. I just needed to talk whether I made sense or not. "I got a phone call that said I needed to stay away from the car parked out in back of my house. It's Mr. Gonzalez's."

"No, we recovered his vehicle."

I shook my head. "No, you didn't. Someone besides me lied to you. His car is parked the back lot right next to mine. Ruby told me where his car was, and I went out to look at it, thinking there may be something in it that would tell us why he was murdered. While I was out there, I got this strange call... it was a mechanical voice telling me to stay away from it. Someone was watching me."

"Did you look inside?"

"No. I ran back into the house."

"Why didn't you call the police?"

"They told me if I did, I'd end up like Mr. Gonzalez."

Adam ran a hand through his silky blond hair, and I could see his aggravation growing.

"So, I was thinking that the package the Thompsons referred to was the car, or something in the car." I continued. "But to backtrack for a second, when I went out for a ride with Jack, he took me to this place way up in the mountains, an overlook on a cliff off a trail that had just been cut. I could see my house. It was the perfect spot for someone to watch me from, and there was garbage up there, as well as an outline of someone lying in the dirt."

"You think someone was watching your house from the ledge?"

"It's a possibility," I said with a shrug. "I also wondered if Jack had something to do with this whole mess. Did he take me up there to give me a warning that people were observing my every movement at home? Or was it a coincidence?"

"Did he say anything to make you think one way or the other?"

I shook my head. "No. But when I realized I could see my house, I got really scared. It may have been my imagination, though."

"Okay. Wow, Bernie."

"I'm not crazy," I said. "You have to believe me."

"Is there anything else?"

I noted he didn't agree or disagree with my proclamation, but I had to convince him I had a full set of marbles.

"Yes. Last night I took Ruby out to the car. She can move through things like doors and walls. She went inside it and didn't see anything except some garbage, but then someone—a man—showed up and chased me into the desert. We went out in the middle of the night, so someone was watching me. They knew I was out by the car."

"Chased you?"

"Well, I'm not sure if he actually ran after me, but he came around to the back lot and stood between the cars and the house, blocking me from heading inside. I ran."

"Did you get a look at him?"

"No," I said, picking up my coffee cup. "It was dark."

"Is that why your face and hands are scratched up?"

"Yes. I was terrified and running for my life."

Well, I thought I was. I didn't even know if my supposed attacker had tried to give chase, or if he just wanted to scare me.

I couldn't meet Adam's gaze as I sipped my java. *Please don't think I'm nuts. Please help me.*

"So, Bernie, who do you think is behind all this?"

"I don't know, Adam. Darla checked him in. Stan argued with him. Sarah poured him the smoothie that had the poison. Jack brought me up to the outlook over my house, which could mean nothing, or it could have been a warning. The Thompsons lied about everything and were talking about 'the package.' It could be any of them, or someone I'm not even aware of."

"Do you think Darla's involved?"

"At first I didn't, but now I'm not sure. She was so mad at me when I gave her name to the police, and now she's furious because she thinks I'm trying to steal Jack away from her. The two aren't related in any way that I can see, but she's not talking to me. Maybe she and Jack are in this together somehow?"

I felt his stare on me and I shifted in my seat. All I

wanted was for someone to believe me, to help me untangle myself from this mess.

"Okay, let's go," Adam said, getting to his feet.

Oh, heck. Was he arresting me?

"W-where are we going?"

"We're heading to the scene of the crime," he replied, sticking out his hand. "Back to your house."

I placed my palm in his and he pulled me off the couch, then reached for his strawberry treat. "I'll eat this on the way."

"What do you want to do at the house?" I asked when we were out on the sidewalk.

"Well, first, I want to meet Ruby."

"You believe me?" I asked, tears welling in my eyes. "That she exists?"

Adam shrugged and took a bite of the pastry. "I don't know. I remember when I was there when you found Mr. Gonzalez, there was something strange going on. Your house felt... different somehow."

"That's her!" I said. "When she's near you, it smells like marijuana and lavender!"

Adam chuckled and shook his head. "I had to arrest her once for marijuana possession. She was out at Cathedral Rock smoking and reading a book."

"That sounds like something she would do."

We continued on our way in comfortable silence. I liked being with Adam, and for the first time since the killing, I felt somewhat safe.

My heart raced as we walked up the pavement to my front door. With shaky hands, I inserted the key and the panel swung open. Taking a deep breath, I walked inside.

I waited for Ruby to make an appearance, but the house remained oddly quiet. Even Elvira didn't show herself.

"Ruby?" I called, setting down my keys. "Can you come out, please?"

Adam slowly strolled around the living room, his arms crossed over his chest as his eyes darted from the ceiling to every corner of the room.

Ruby came rushing down the stairs, the purple mumu swirling around her legs. "Oh, thank goodness!" she yelled. "We have to get out of here, Bernie!"

"What's going on?" I asked, my voice dropping to almost a whisper as fear clenched my throat.

"Up there!" Ruby shouted, pointing to the second floor. "There's a man hiding upstairs!"

CHAPTER 19

I slowly backed up toward the front door, my heart thundering, my hands shaking. Someone was in my house?

"What's going on?" Adam said, hurrying over to me. "What happened?"

"Ruby says there's a man upstairs," I whispered.

Adam's eyes widened as he unclipped his gun safety on the holster. "Who is it?"

I turned to Ruby, who now stood next to me.

"I don't know. He's got a ski mask on," she said. "I tried to scare him, but every time I rushed him, he started sneezing. My guess is he's allergic to lavender. He's not going anywhere."

"She says he's got a ski mask on," I said. "She can't identify him."

"What room is he in?" Adam asked, his gaze focused on the staircase.

"First door on the right," Ruby replied. "The room

where Gonzalez died."

I repeated Ruby's answer, and Adam nodded.

"How did he get in?" I whispered.

"Through the back door," Ruby said. "He broke the window, turned the knob, and waltzed right in."

Adam glanced at me expectantly, and I parroted Ruby once again.

"Bernie, I'm going to call for backup, which means there'll be at least a half-dozen cops here again," he said. "Then, I'm going to go upstairs and take down that guy. I don't want to shoot him, but I will. Chances are someone is going to be hurt. So if this is some type of prank, you need to tell me right now."

"It's not," I said, tears welling in my eyes as I wrung my hands. "I swear to you, I'm not crazy and I have no idea who is up there."

He studied me a moment, then nodded. "You need to wait outside," he whispered as he opened the front door. "Head out into the street. In fact, get away from the building. There's only one reason why someone would be in your house, and that's to hold up their promise of killing you."

"Oh, heavens," Ruby yelled, throwing her hands up in the air. "If I weren't dead, I'd be having a coronary right now!"

"Not so fast," a deep voice said from the top of the stairs. The figure, dressed in black from head to toe, was pointing a gun at us. His voice sounded unnatural, as if he were trying to disguise it. "Nobody leaves."

I stared at him as he strode down the staircase, both

terrified for my life and horrified I didn't recognize him. Who was it?

Three men had been on my list of suspects: Jack, Stan, and Bob Thompson. Unfortunately, all were built similarly and my intruder wasn't speaking in his normal voice. Being covered head-to-toe in black didn't allow for me to notice any distinct features.

Adam's hand inched slowly down to his gun and rested on the handle. "Put down the weapon," he ordered, his voice strong. "I don't want to hurt you."

"You won't hurt me," the attacker said. "So, I'm going to explain exactly what's going to happen."

"Put. Down. Your. Weapon," Adam said again, his voice having taken a deadly tone. "I *will* shoot you."

The man raised his gun and pointed it in my direction. Ruby moved in front of me, as if her ghostly form could stop a bullet. "As I was saying, here's what's going to happen. You two are going to sit down on that couch and stay there."

"Don't do it!" Ruby screamed. "He'll shoot you once he gains compliance!"

"He might shoot if we don't comply," I muttered.

"What did you say?" the gunman asked.

"Nothing. Sorry. Talking to myself. I do that when I'm upset, anxious and having my life threatened."

His beady eyes stared at me through the small slits in the facemask. "Sit down, you annoying troll."

While I didn't appreciate being referred to as a troll, I hurried over to the couch and took a seat with Adam trailing right behind me.

"Why doesn't Adam just shoot him?" Ruby said, standing face-to-face with the attacker. "Why is he sitting there like you just invited him for tea on a Sunday afternoon?"

I glanced over at Adam, and didn't see what Ruby described at all. Beads of sweat dotted his upper lip, his breath shallow. He still had his hand on his weapon. Maybe he was waiting for the right time to make a move?

"Put your gun and the radio on the table, copper," the intruder said. "And no funny business, or I'll give old nosey a third eye."

That would be me. The nosey troll. The insults simply kept getting worse.

Adam carefully slid both onto the table, then sat back against the cushions.

"You have to keep him talking, Bernie," Ruby said. "They never shoot when they're talking."

Geez. How many times had she been held at gunpoint?

"If it's who I think it may be, he'll want to tell you how clever he is," Ruby continued as she walked around him. "I wish I could grab this hood off him. I'd smash his face in and—"

"I know who you are," I lied. "If you're going to kill me, you might as well tell me what's in the car and why you murdered Mr. Gonzalez."

"Really? You think you know me? I don't believe you," he asked.

"It's obvious," I said with a shrug. "I figured it out. I

just need to know why you murdered him."

"A little situation got out of control. I think he may have been trying to steal my business."

Okay, who owned businesses in my suspect list? Almost everyone. Dang it!

"That wasn't very nice of him," I ventured. "The product can't be as good as yours."

He chuckled and shook his head. "That remains to be seen. Now shut up while I think of what I'm going to do with your bodies. Maybe a murder-suicide will work best here. Secret lovers or something like that."

I exchanged glances with Adam and noted neither of us were too keen on the idea.

"Keep him talking! He can't talk and think at the same time!" Ruby yelled.

"You were using the overlook to watch the car, weren't you?" I asked. "At least tell me I'm right about that."

"Oh, you were right," he said, his voice deep and gruff. "It's the perfect spot to keep an eye on the car."

"So you saw me go out last night."

"I did, but not from the ledge. I was watching the house from the street. It was pure luck I walked around the back to find you."

What horrible timing. If I'd waited an hour, or gone out earlier, he may not have noticed. Not that it had done any good. I still wouldn't have known what was in the vehicle.

"Why didn't you just take the car right after you killed him?" I asked. "Wouldn't that have been easier?"

"It would have, except he didn't follow the plan. He was supposed to leave town after getting the smoothie and die on the road, but he didn't. Instead, he died here and I didn't have the keys to the car. I figured I had at least a twelve-hour window to sneak in and grab them. I didn't think you'd disturb him until it was time for him to check-out, but you found him early and called the cops."

Wow. I really foiled the grand-master plan without even realizing it. Well, Ruby had. I never would have barged in on Gonzalez except for Ruby mentioning he was dead.

He lowered the gun to his side and tilted his head. "Why did you go into his room?"

My intruder was just as confused about it as the police had been. I glanced at Adam and then at Ruby. Did I tell him about her?

I marveled at the way he continually altered his voice, yet, I felt I knew him, which meant that my original suspect list had been correct.

"I foiled his plot!" Ruby squealed. "It's probably a good thing, or you would have had a stranger in your house, which would have been very dangerous for you."

"What's in the car?" Adam asked.

The attacker raised the gun again, this time aiming it at Adam. I shut my eyes for a moment. The thought of Adam not making it through this was so upsetting, I wanted to throw up.

"It's none of your business, copper."

Something in the way he spoke resonated with me and I stared him down. After a moment, he lowered his weapon again. I reached over and squeezed Adam's hand, hoping he got the message that I was about to deliver his chance to take down the murderer. Well, if my plan worked. Honestly, I was relying on a lot of shock value and hoping I'd guessed correctly.

"Ruby, who do you think this guy is?" I asked loudly, turning toward the front door as if I spoke to someone standing there. "I believe you have a name for me."

The intruder's gaze flickered from the door and back to me.

"Ruby?" he muttered. "She's dead. What the heck is wrong with you?"

"Yes, she is," I said quietly. "Except, she's not. Her ghost is here. She told me she never liked you... Stan."

I slowly stood, praying I was correct. "In fact, she's right behind you, ready to make your life miserable."

The intruder turned around and in one swift movement, Adam jumped on the coffee table and lunged off it, landing on the gunman.

They wrestled and Ruby stood over them cheering Adam on. "Get him, copper! Don't let this jerk win! Dang, I love a good fistfight!"

Adam slammed the attacker's hand down on the floor and the gun skidded away. I hurried over to pick it up, then grabbed Adam's weapon and ran into the kitchen. After I hid both under the sink, I returned to the fight, ready to jump in if necessary, but thankfully, Adam had subdued him.

And I'd been right.

Adam pulled off the mask to reveal Stan and his bloody nose.

As Adam cuffed him, Stan glared at me with such hatred, I wilted under his gaze and a chill of fear washed over me. But it was over. I was no longer in danger. I plopped down on the couch and sighed in relief the stress and fear oozed from me and tears tracked down my cheeks.

"Let's hear the story from the beginning," Adam said, helping Stan to sit upright. "Tell us everything."

I listened intently as the man told his tale.

He'd been selling marijuana for years out of As the Pins Drop, and I remembered Ruby mentioning it when I visited him that day. There had been rumors someone else may be moving into town to give him some competition, and Stan had been on the lookout. He did have a driving altercation with Mr. Gonzalez on the freeway, and they'd actually pulled over and exchange words. That was when Stan smelled the drugs in the car and decided to take them in case he'd found his competitor. However, he also knew that the highway through Arizona was one drug smugglers used frequently and he couldn't leave Gonzalez alive, or he might have a cartel after him. Besides, he needed to teach Gonzalez, a horrible driver, a lesson. What better way to do that than to grab his product?

When Gonzalez pulled into town, Stan realized he had the opportunity to throw together a plan.

He followed him to Sarah's Sensational Smoothies, but the car was locked. Since Stan was dating Sarah, he was allowed in the back. With so many customers out front, Sarah had brought back smoothies to blend with the extra mixer. When he realized she had Jose's, he waited for her to deliver some of the completed smoothies up front and offered to help with the mixing. Then, he slipped rat poison and some of Sarah's pain medication into Jose's cup, which he found on the shelf and in her purse. Stan planned to follow Jose out of town, wait for him to pull over on the side of the highway, and then steal the drugs.

But instead of heading out of town, Gonzalez drove to my bed and breakfast. Stan tried to run him out of the area and back to the highway by confronting him yet again in front of my place, but his plan failed, and Gonzalez died in my house.

"I thought I could at least grab his drugs," Stan said. "I was going to break in late that night to get his keys, but I saw the cops at your house and knew he'd died. I thought I could still get the drugs... I just needed the keys."

"Then you called us and reported his vehicle," Adam said. "The vehicle that wasn't his."

"Yes. I even forged the registration. I was waiting for the right moment to get his real car. Waiting for things to die down."

"And you watched my house," I muttered.

"Yeah, I did," Stan spat. "You have been nothing but trouble for me, Bernadette Maxwell. Sticking your nose where it doesn't belong all the darn time. Just like your crazy grandmother."

He glanced around as if waiting for the wrath of Ruby to descend. She stood behind him and smacked his head. Unfortunately, her ghostly hand moved right through the brainless wonder.

"Are the drugs in the car?" Adam asked. "Why didn't you just break a window?"

"It's alarmed," Stan muttered. "I didn't want to cause a scene, especially when no one knew the drugs were in there. If the alarm went off, it would draw attention to the car and me. I could have probably gotten away with stealing the drugs, but I was afraid someone would see me do it."

But Ruby had been inside the car and hadn't seen anything. "How were they hidden?" I asked.

Stan didn't answer, but stared at the floor, thoroughly defeated. I grinned at his misery while Adam and I retrieved the weapons in the kitchen and returned to the living room. He spoke on his phone in low tones while Ruby and I watched Stan.

"I told you this man was stupid," Ruby said.

"Yes, you did tell me that about him," I said, staring at my intruder.

"Who told what about me?" he asked glancing around the room once again.

I leaned my elbows on my knees and sat forward.

"Ruby told me you were dumb. I was just agreeing with her."

Stan stared at me a moment as the color drained from his face. I could see him trying to put together the timeline between when I'd arrived in town, and when she'd died. He was unable to, which could only mean I was crazy or I was talking to a ghost. Either one should rattle him.

The front door opened and Sheriff Walker walked in.

"Everything's under control, sir," Adam said. "I've got a full confession and a shipment of drugs, possibly from a Mexican cartel."

"Wow. Nice work, Adam. That means a lot of paperwork for you, but it's a great bust."

And my life was no longer in danger.

Ruby glided over to me and grinned. "Now that you're safe, does that mean we can have our dance party?"

CHAPTER 20

*T*wo days later, I felt a little more like myself. Sleep will do that for a person. It was also nice not to be glancing over my shoulder every few minutes, wondering if and when I was going to be murdered.

So, with my life back in order, it was time for a dance party.

Ruby led me to an attic area above the last bedroom on the right I didn't realize existed. She showed me how to get to it through the closet, climbing a small ladder and hoisting myself up into the space where I found her trunks full of costumes, which we used to wear for our dance parties when I was little.

"I had no idea these were still around," I said, opening one and finding a white feather boa. I removed it and placed it around my neck. When I was little, I always felt so grown up when wearing it and the sweet memory made me smile.

"When you didn't come to visit anymore, I decided to put them away," Ruby said as she floated around the small space. "Had to hire a handyman to help me get them up here."

Guilt washed through me once again and I sighed.

"Oh, jeez, Bernie," Ruby huffed. "Stop beating yourself up. You had a life to live and a mother telling you I was bad news. I was sad when you didn't come to visit, but I understood."

I nodded and pulled out a pair of sequined pants. Ruby used to wear them during our disco parties. "Do you still have the disco ball?"

"Of course. I think it's in that trunk over there."

I opened the lid and found it in perfect condition.

"You know, those used to be called Myriad Reflectors. They were around in the 1920s."

"I didn't realize that," I said, holding it above my head. "I think disco ball is a much better name."

"Agreed. Myriad Reflector sounds like a medical device."

We watched as little lights reflected around the room from the setting sun coming through the small window.

"What do you think?" I asked, setting it down. "A disco party?"

"Sure! I always loved pretending I was dancing with John Travolta in Saturday Night Fever giving him a run for his money in hip thrusts."

"Oh, he was good in that, wasn't he?"

"So sexy!" Ruby exclaimed. "I wish I could slip into those sequined pants. I looked pretty hot in them."

And she had. I set them down and stared at her. "Ruby, we talked about it briefly, but why are you stuck here?"

"I don't know," she replied with a shrug. "Dying was pretty jarring. I remember going to the light in the tunnel and hearing voices, but I was too confused to pay them any attention. I didn't hear what they said to me."

"Have you tried to go to the light since then?"

Ruby nodded. "It's an endless walk. I never get any closer."

"Can you think about it?" I asked. "Try to remember what was said?"

"Sure. I'll give it some more thought."

"We need to get you to your final resting place," I said quietly.

"You tired of having me around?"

"Of course not. It's just… it doesn't feel fair to you. You can't do the things you used to love while alive. You're stuck in this place where you've become an observer."

"It's not so bad, Bernie. Especially now that you see me."

I smiled, wishing I could hug her. "You can't wear these pants," I said, holding up the sequin slacks. "You can't have a shot of tequila. You can't smoke or ride an ATV by yourself."

"And don't forget the men," Ruby said. "I can't have fun with any men."

"That's true," I replied, laughing.

"You're right. My situation is just awful," Ruby said, plopping down on the floor next to me. "Maybe I do need to figure out why I'm stuck here."

"We can do that together," I said.

"Let's worry about that later," Ruby said. "For now, let's get you dressed up, hang that ball in the living room, and blast some Bee Gees!"

AFTER WE MOVED the couches back, I hung the disco ball from the chandelier. I still had Ruby's old record player and a box of albums tucked away in the garage. We rifled through them until we found the Bee Gees.

"Look at that!" Ruby said. "Perfect condition!"

I hauled everything inside, set it up, and connected the record player to the speakers, then poured myself a glass of wine. After I slipped on the sequined pants, we were ready to party.

"Dance party!" Ruby yelled as *You Should Be Dancing* screamed through the speakers.

Even though she'd been seventy-seven when she died, Ruby still had all the moves. With her hips swaying, she busted out John Travolta's epic steps, the Bus Stop, and a few I didn't recognize. It had always been easy pretending the living room was a disco and now was no different than it had been when she was alive.

We moved down the middle of it together doing the Hand Jive while in fits of giggles.

Throughout the fun, I couldn't help but consider why Ruby was stuck on this side. What had happened during her travels to the light to keep her here? Why couldn't she move on, and why could I see her now, but not for the previous three years?

Had the powers that be struck me with lightning so I would notice her? If so, for what purpose? Surely not because they wanted me to have dance parties with her.

Both of us fell on the couch when the music ended. Elvira stared at us with a critical eye. I wished she'd wasn't so serious and she would lighten up a bit. But then I realized my cat had my personality. It had taken a ghost and almost being murdered for me to relax. I wondered if a little catnip may help the feline.

The knock at the front door startled us all, and I stood to answer.

"Tell them to go away!" Ruby yelled after me. "We're busy!"

I waved at her over my shoulder, having no intention of allowing anyone inside. I just wanted to see who it was.

When I glanced through the peephole, I stood in utter shock when I saw Adam. Without thinking, I flung open the door. His smile faded as he glanced at me from head to toe.

"Let me guess," I said while trying to smooth out my tangled hair. "Sequins aren't your thing?"

He shoved his hands into his jean pockets and shook his head. "No. Sequins are good. Just haven't seen any since the last time I watched Saturday Night Fever."

I laughed and grabbed his hand. "Not only do we have sequins, but a disco ball as well."

Instead of running away, Adam followed me into the living room and nodded as he watched the little lights travel around the room. "I'm impressed," he said, grinning.

"Oh, heck," Ruby said from the couch. "Not the fuzz. Not now."

I ignored her and led Adam over to the opposite couch from where Ruby lounged. "Thanks. We were having a disco dance party. We used to do it all the time when I was young and came to visit."

"We… meaning you and Ruby?" Adam asked.

"Yes." My heart sank as he glanced around the room, his lips pursed as if unsure what to say. Maybe he was going to tell me he thought I was crazy and didn't want to date me. I wouldn't blame him because I still questioned my sanity every now and then.

"I… I… uh, came by to tell you that we've got the Gonzalez case totally wrapped up," Adam said. "The drugs were hidden in the doors. When we finally gained entrance to the car, we could smell it, but it took a minute to actually find the packages."

"Very sneaky," I said.

"Yes. We even looked into the Thompsons just to

cover all our bases. You were right—they weren't clean."

"What were they doing in town?" I asked.

Adam sighed and rubbed his forehead. "The package was a case of stolen phones. One of those fell-off-the-back-of-the-truck deals. They weren't up to any good."

"At least they weren't trafficking kids or something horrible like that," Ruby said, shaking her head. "Look for the silver linings."

I nodded absently then turned to Adam. He'd been watching me.

"What did she say?" he asked.

"She said she's glad they were stealing phones instead of trafficking kids."

"That's a good way to look at it."

"Silver linings," I murmured.

While Adam rubbed his hands together, I got the distinct impression he was terribly uncomfortable.

"What's wrong?" I asked.

"Well, I was also wondering if you wanted to go hiking tomorrow, and there's something else… but I feel very weird talking about it."

With a grin, I nodded, thrilled that he wanted to spend time with me. "A hike sounds great, and I know what you mean. Coming to you with my story about Ruby was one of the hardest things I'd ever done. Thank you for believing me and not laughing at me or taking me to an insane asylum."

Adam smiled, but I could see he was still uncomfortable.

"If I can tell you that, I would think whatever you have to say would be easy," I added with a chuckle.

"Well, here's the deal. I've thought my place was haunted for a long time. It just feels like there's someone there."

I'd never in a million years expected him to take the conversation in that direction. Did he honestly just tell me he thought he had a ghost?

I glanced over at Ruby who had sprung to her feet and hurried over to us. She stood right in front of Adam. "Ask him who he thinks it is."

"Who is it?" I said, finding the whole matter a bit unbelievable. For a brief moment, I considered he might be messing with me, attempting to play some type of trick, and he hadn't believed me about Ruby.

"I don't know, but I was wondering if you and Ruby could come to my house? Maybe you two can see whoever it is and find out what they want?"

He seemed serious. He was either a really good actor or he was telling the truth.

I'd just gotten used to my own ghost. Did I want to tangle with another one? And what if Adam's was evil, instead of someone like silly and harmless Ruby?

"Please?" he begged. "I sometimes feel like I'm losing my mind. Stuff gets moved around and I can smell cigars at times. I don't smoke them. I've ignored it for long enough, and I really need some help, Bernie."

How was I supposed to say no to that?

I met Ruby's stare and she shook her head. "We have to help him," she said.

My gut tightened at the idea, but she was right.

Did Adam truly have a ghost, and if so, who was it and why was it trapped on this side?

***

To find out who Adam's ghost is and to join Ruby and Bernie on their next mystery, please grab The Tourist is Toast today!

If you're wondering about Bernadette's accident where she was hit by lightning, you'll want to dive into the complete series, the Tri-Town Murders.

Don't forget to check out Dearly Departed, a 1960s cozy mystery! Patty Briggs is living her best life as a stewardess, until she finds her neighbor dead!

The Tri-Town Murders

Complete Series

Follow newspaper reporter Tilly and her group of fun, quirky friends as they solve murders in a fictional, small town in California.

News and Nectarines

News and Nachos

News and Nutmeg

News and Noodles

Killer Skies Mysteries

Set in 1965, join Patty Briggs, stewardess extraordinaire, as she flies the skies and solves murders with the help of her friends… and one cute FBI agent!

ABOUT THE AUTHOR

Carly Winter is the pen name for a USA Today best-selling and award-winning romance author.

When not writing, she enjoys spending time with her family, reading and enjoying the fantastic Arizona weather (except summer - she doesn't like summer). She does like dogs, wine and chocolate and wishes Christmas happened twice a year.

To be sign up for her newsletter and be notified of new releases, book recommendations, to learn more about Carly and for your chance to win giveaways, please see her website: CarlyWinterCozyMysteries.com